When Sisterhood Was in Flower

Also by Florence King

Southern Ladies and Gentlemen
Wasp, Where Is Thy Sting?
He: An Irreverent Look at the American Male

When Sisterhood Was in Flower

Florence
King

The Viking Press   New York

Library of Congress Cataloging in Publication Data
King, Florence.
    When sisterhood was in flower.
    I. Title.
PS3561.I4754W47   813'.54   81-65284
ISBN 0-670-75998-8   AACR2

A portion of this book originally appeared in *Penthouse* in slightly different form.

Grateful acknowledgment is made to W. W. Norton & Company, Inc., for permission to reprint a selection by la Rochefoucauld from *The Norton Anthology of World Masterpieces, Continental Edition*, Fourth Ed., p. 1079. Copyright © 1980 by W. W. Norton & Company, Inc. Edited by Maynard Mack et al.

Printed in the United States of America
Set in Video Compano

For my editor, Amanda Vaill

Co-founder, with the author,
of the Daughters of the War of Jenkins' Ear

When
Sisterhood
Was in
Flower

1

She belonged to the Short Skirts League, as a matter of course; for she belonged to any and every league that had been founded for almost any purpose whatever.

—Henry James, *The Bostonians*

Call me Isabel.

The story of how I was shanghaied into the feminist movement begins in Boston in the politically pulsating year of 1971. I was not pulsating. Except for wishing that someone would appoint Ayn Rand Secretary of HEW, my progressive fire remained unlit. You may as well know, before you get any further into this, that my politics were and still are Royalist; I believe in absolute monarchy and the divine right of kings. One thing I like about Bloody Mary's philosophy of government: she never said a word about lung cancer.

I felt out of place, to put it mildly, amid the Harvard SDS *zeitgeist*, but having sprung from a family that has lived in Virginia since 1672, I decided that I needed to live up North to engage in what writers call "gathering new experiences." I kept waiting for the liberal protest spirit to benefit me professionally, but it did not. With mind closed and legs open, all I gathered was lovers.

I am a native of Queen Caroline Court House (the Virginia way of designating a county seat), a Tidewater hamlet on lower Chesapeake Bay named for George IV's consort, Caroline of Brunswick, who is best remembered for refusing to change her underdrawers. "She stank," wrote Lord Malmesbury, with admirable aristocratic bluntness, in his diary. One of his extant letters containing the same observation is proudly displayed in our town library as a tribute to the complacency of our patroness.

The Queen's attachment to the tried and true was shared by everyone in town, and especially by my grandmother, who refused to use a telephone. She communicated with calling cards, turning down the corners this way or that with such Druidic expertise that she could say *I am at home on Thursday but will be out of town over the weekend attending a funeral* without writing a word.

A firm believer in the theory that if time had any decency it would stand still, she liked to set a good example for it by appearing in historical *tableaux vivants* at Colonial Dames soirées. Dressed in full farthingale to represent the Spirit of Old Virginia, she would march out to a drum roll, strike a suitable pose, and freeze in place.

Freezing in place was the cornerstone of all Granny's thinking, which is undoubtedly why my mind-broadening move North did not work. One of her many definitions of a lady was someone who died in the same house, in the same room, in the same bed in which she had been born—and, though she didn't spell it out, conceived. Her fixation on stay-put living was such that she must have found it grimly fitting when my mother went her one better and died at the table. It happened when I was eight. In an attempt to talk, laugh, and eat all at the same time in the manner of sprightly Southern belles, she swallowed a bone.

My father took little notice of Mama's demise because it had nothing to do with the *Titanic.* Genteelly referred to as his hobby, his interest in the great sea tragedy was actually a textbook case of monomania of the most degenerative kind; as far as he was concerned, anything that had happened after 2:20 a.m., April 15, 1912, had not really happened. In a steady-on-course progression toward madness, he filled the house with ship models, drawings, and an exact-to-scale diagram of the fatal slit, which several people mistook for a vulva; recited the entire passenger list from memory; and whistled "Nearer, My God, To Thee" while he shaved.

All this left little time for work. Ostensibly, he was president and general manager of the cardboard container manufacturing firm he inherited from his family. A profitable business in anyone else's hands, it started sinking as soon as Daddy took the helm. He insisted on making far more hat boxes than the modern American woman needed, and spent most of his and his secretary's office time corresponding with other *Titanic* freaks, an eerily formal lot who used "Esquire" and "Your obedient servant" and held what has to be the quaintest élitist prejudice of all time: they snubbed the *Lusitania* as an upstart shipwreck because it resulted from an act of man instead of an Act of God.

The other member of our household was Mama's younger sister, Aunt Edna, who worked as secretary to the rector of St. Jude the Impossible, Episcopal, but whose real career was having cramps. The whole town knew about Aunt Edna's female trouble. She recited her complete gynecological history to anyone who would listen, made bets on when her irregular menses would start, and somehow connived to get three paid sick leave days a month from her boss, Father Chillingsworth, who personally interceded with the bishop on the subject of her delicate parts and kept a record of her period on his Canterbury desk calendar with all the other movable feasts. Once, he got it mixed up with Easter and wore the wrong vestments.

After Mama died, Granny took over my raising and the long battle for my mind began. Her chief task, as she saw it, was to break me of all unfeminine habits so I would not end up like Mrs. Roosevelt. The most unfeminine thing a girl could do, in her opinion, was become a "bluestocking," as she called female intellectuals, so when it developed that I loved to read, she set out to separate me from books with every weapon in her arsenal.

First she explained what happened to little girls who read too much.

"Your eyes will fall out. They'll just fall right out and go plop at your feet. You'll end up on a street corner with a white cane and a little tin cup. I can just see you going tap-tap-tap with your cane and rattling your poor little cup. People will say, 'There's that poor little girl who wouldn't listen to her grandmother, and now look at her with those big black glasses over her poor little empty sockets.' "

When that didn't work, she tried the blood-poisoning argument.

"If you read a book when you have a cut on your finger, the ink will enter your bloodstream and go all through your system, and when it reaches your heart, you'll die. You'll just fall down dead. People will say, 'That was the poor little girl who died while reading. The ink killed her.' "

Only Granny could reduce the flower of Western culture to the status of an air bubble. The more she nagged, the more I read, the more she nagged. Matters came to a head when I was seventeen; I told her I wanted to be a writer.

"You're going to end up just like That Woman!" she cried. "Next thing I know, you'll be going down in a coal mine! Why don't you just go whole hog and buy your-

self a suit of armor like that Joan of Arc? She was a mor-
phodite, you know—I have it on good authority.
Kissypoo Carmichael did a paper on her for the women's
club. Mark my words, you'll wind up in the insane asy-
lum if you try to go against nature. Mental exertion rav-
ages the female organs, too. You'll have trouble down
below if you don't watch out. You know what they always say: a whistling woman and a crowing hen always
come to a tragic end."

College is supposed to be a time of growth and discov-
ery. Granny, of course, did not want me to go, but I insisted, so in keeping with her definition of compromise, I
was enrolled in St. Mary Star of the Sea Episcopal College for Women, a small, select grave of academe located
on lower Chesapeake Bay in the town of Queen Caroline
Court House. It was three blocks from home, so I kept on
walking to school the same as before.

Although I was a student of the sixties, my only contact with campus turmoil was the evening news. The
closest St. Mary Star ever came to a riot was the time a
mouse joined us for Evensong, and the nearest thing to a
controversy was a hushed argument over whether
"Bread of Angels" could be sung as *"Panis Angelicus."* The
high-church element prevailed as usual, so we sang it in
Latin. Had any days of rage erupted in our Anglican en-
clave, we would have referred to them as *"dies irae."* The
local crab fishermen didn't call us softshell Catholics for
nothing.

To prepare for a writing career, I majored in literature
and took all of the many zero-growth courses that St.
Mary Star offered, such as advanced Latin, the Augustan
Essay, the English Rural Novel ("Eee, by goom, thart's
summat"), and Tragedy 303, an intensive seminar in the
plays of Racine in which we were forbidden to speak
except in alexandrine verse. It was taught by Miss Dalrymple, who was Kissypoo Carmichael's adopted half-
sister, a relationship so fraught with bend sinisters,

wrong-sided blankets, and double cousinships that Miss Dalrymple was said to commit incest every time she took a douche.

I graduated from St. Mary Star qualified to do nothing except crossword puzzles in ink and play Rhyming Sam in a traveling carnival, so I took a stenotype course at Queen Caroline Business School. I thought being a court reporter would be a good way to gather experience for writing, but no Lizzie Bordens or Black Dahlias came my way. Instead I took boundary disputes, apocalyptic Southern-style car wrecks, and divorcing good ole boys who broke down on the witness stand and sobbed, "I'll love her till the ocean wears rubber pants to keep its bottom dry!"

When I had been working a few weeks, my father wrote a note saying "I hate this century" and shot himself. The next month, Granny died in the cemetery, felled by a heat stroke as she was trying to read the worn inscription on a seventeenth-century tombstone to see if it belonged to one of her ancestors. "She formed a Cross on the grave," said Father Chillingsworth in his eulogy.

I had the choice of staying home and menstruating with Aunt Edna, or striking out to gather experience, so I left and headed North. I tried New York first, but it affected me the way mention of Eleanor Roosevelt affected Granny, so I pressed on to Boston, where I made the mistake of renting an apartment in Cambridge that turned out to be next door to the Hari Krishna headquarters. It was an experience I preferred not to gather, so I moved out and tried Beacon Hill because I thought people like George Apley still lived there.

I had been living in the new place about a week when I crossed paths with Polly Bradshaw.

What was to be my last day of peace and quiet started with a trip to the post office. I emerged from my apartment on the misnamed Joy Street to mail my latest manuscript, "Beloved Rake," to Moth and Flame Regency Romances. It was my fifth sale to the brooding-and-riding-crop genre and by now I had a method down pat. I wrote them on the stenotype machine while I was drunk and transcribed them when I was sober. In case you're interested,

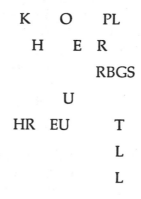

means "Come here, you little fool."

As I walked into the post office at Government Center, my manuscript was scorched by a boy whose flaming draft card had got out of control. He gave me a sign—peace or the finger, I couldn't tell which—and returned to his sleeping bag. On the other side of the plaza, a group of Gay Liberationists chanted "Two, four, six, eight, we don't overpopulate," and a person of uncertain gender wearing a Halloween skeleton costume marched up and down with a sign that read REMEMBER KENT STATE.

I mailed the manuscript and started back home. As I was crossing the plaza, a strange intense girl in tie-dyed bell bottoms and Mao jacket rushed up and kissed me.

"I love you," she whispered. "Pass it on. If everybody says it to everybody else, we can forge a chain of love to stretch around the world."

I peeled her off me and crossed the street. On the

corner I was stopped by a boy wearing a placard that read SAVE A TREE. He held out a flowerpot containing a pathetic pine seedling.

"This is a tree. Do you know what trees do for you? Man, they're the best friends you've got. Like they breathe for you, you know? Like they work their ass off for you! Got any spare change? It's not for me, it's for the trees."

I evaded him and trudged on up the Joy Street hill, picking my way through dog droppings and spacy college students in floppy felt hats decorated with *Richard Nixon Is a Lesbian* buttons. They were just standing there hugging themselves, but as I drew abreast they came to life with a vengeance. Lips curled, and a boy clenched his fist and shook it at me.

"Reactionary!"

How did he know? I wasn't wearing anything expensive, just a plaid skirt and a sweater set with a single strand of cultured pearls. This sort of thing was always happening to me since I had moved North, like the time in New York when I was called for jury duty and the defense attorney took one look at me and said "Challenge." Defiantly, I tossed my head at the students and walked the rest of the way up the hill to my building.

As I mounted the steps, I ran into the landlord, Vittorio Gioppi, known to his tenants as Gioppi the Woppi. The soubriquet had been started by the Martinellis in 2B, who claimed he gave Italians a bad name, and quickly spread through the halls like the recent fire in another one of his buildings.

When he saw me, he tried to conceal the crumpled paper bag he held. It was very full but not at all heavy, which meant that he was on another lightbulb-stealing mission. Whenever the tenants in one of his buildings complained that their hall lights had gone out, he would sneak into another one and rip off the bulbs.

"Hey, you seen any hippies around here?" he asked me.

"They're all over the place."

"Nah, I mean on the premises here."

He waved grandly at the two scabrous row houses that were laughably affixed with little brass plates long gone to green that read *Tradesmen and Servants Enter in Rear.* We had hand-painted carriage blocks, too. One said *fuck* and the other said *suck.*

Gioppi squared his ovoid shoulders proudly. "I'm talkin' about Commie bums that wanna destroy our American Way of Life. Last night at the V.F.W., somebody told me there was a bunch of them Weathermen camped out somewhere on the Hill. If you see 'em, call me right away, hear? We gotta stop them creeps. My buddies and me wanna capture 'em singlehanded so we can go to Washington and get hard hats from President Nixon."

He laid a hand over his heart, his fingers caressing his rhinestone-studded American flag pin.

"I got *my* Plymouth Rock right here. My grandmother, rest her soul, wasn't in no D.A.R., but I love my country more than life."

He had seen Granny's picture in full battle regalia the day I moved in, so it was meant as a dig. One of these days I was going to tell him that my grandmother wasn't in no D.A.R. either. Like many members of Colonial Dames, she looked down on the Daughters and frequently referred to them as Johnny-come-latelies because they required ancestors who went no further back than 1776.

Gioppi got into his car, which was plastered with flag decals and patriotic bumper stickers, including *Support Your Local Police; Register Communists, Not Firearms; Remember the Pueblo;* and *Put Your Heart in America Or Get Your* [picture of a donkey] *Out.* As I watched him drive off, I thought how comforting patriotism must be.

I entered the building and climbed up to the top-floor studio I had just rented. It was unremarkable in every way except for a pink marble fireplace. Naturally, the fireplace was no longer functional, but it was a shining jewel in Gioppi's otherwise tarnished crown, and a pleasant reminder of the days when Beacon Hill's favorite George had been Apley instead of Jackson.

The room had been part of a huge turn-of-the-century bedroom which Gioppi had divided into two cell-like apartments by tacking up a piece of fiberboard to make a wall. It was only slightly thicker than paper but so far there had been no noise problem. Whoever lived next door was hardly ever home; I heard nothing except an occasional dull thwacking sound.

I took off my good clothes and got into a pair of jeans and a Fork Union Military Academy sweatshirt that had belonged to an old beau. I mixed a strong drink, lowered myself carefully into Gioppi's sprung arm chair, and lit a cigarette. Granny gazed in disapproval from her silver frame. Not because I was smoking and drinking—tobacco and bourbon are Southern vices, after all—but because I was wearing jeans. They had been grounds for expulsion at St. Mary Star, but even that anachronism paled before Granny's standards: she used to put on her hat to go out and get the mail.

I turned on the TV, but there was nothing on except soaps and a local PBS feminist talk show called "Heated Topics." I had never watched it but I had read about it in the papers. It was so controversial that it started with a viewer-discretion warning and ended with a disclaimer. Despite these cautionary measures, they had been thrown off the air a few times. The last show to cause trouble was the one on do-it-yourself gynecological examinations, when they all started looking up each other's twats and turning their Isles of McGillicuddy to the camera. If there had been any horses left to frighten, "Heated Topics" would have caused a stampede.

Having just finished writing a Regency, I couldn't take the soaps, so I decided to watch the feminists.

While all the cautions and warnings and no-nos were on I got up and fixed another drink and returned in time to be greeted by the moderator. She had long red hair parted in the middle and hanging down in the usual feminist style, a bony face full of freckles, and one of those long, lean Yankee builds. She wore a little Mother Bloor number that passed for a dress.

"Hello, I'm Polly Bradshaw," she began, in a chowdery Boston accent. "This afternoon we continue our twenty-part series on alternative choices. On our last show we discussed natural childbirth. Our guest today is going to tell us about a really *super* natural way to have a baby. Would you please welcome Ms. Grace Garrison-Talbot, president of the Birth Bucket League of America."

Ms. Garrison-Talbot came on stage rolling a large clay urn on its rim like a spare tire. She wore her hair in a top-knot stuck with a leather hat pin and a T-shirt inscribed *Get Back on the Can!* She took a chair across from Polly Bradshaw, righted the urn, patted it fondly, and began her spiel.

"This is a birth bucket, used for centuries by women before *male* physicians conspired to make us give birth in a prone position."

The slide toward feminist English had begun.

"When did the birth bucket originate?" asked Polly Bradshaw.

It was a fatal question; feminists can always trace anything back to a dry Atlantis. Ms. Garrison-Talbot was no different. She launched into a tribute to the good *old* days, when every country was a matriarchy and the world was full of wonderfully well-adjusted people who chewed on umbilical cords like beef jerky and were so happy that they neglected to leave anything to posterity except the shards of their old birth buckets.

Next came the standard tribute to those daredevil

Celtic warrior queens with names like Fellatrix, who filled their birth buckets during pit stops at the chariot races. She finished with the tragic tale of somebody named Elspeth of Thuringa, who committed suicide in 1274 after her birth bucket was stolen from under her by a band of monks.

"Our Judo-Christian heritage," Polly Bradshaw malapropped, her voice bleak.

"Now, I know what your first question is," said Ms. Garrison-Talbot. "Everybody always asks it. You must be worried about the baby's soft spot."

I was worried about hers. She turned the birth bucket on its side so the camera could pick up the interior.

"You have to put something soft in the bottom for the baby to land in. Ancient Egyptian women used crocodile dung. It's not available here in Massachusetts, but if you plan to give birth in the Gulf Coast area, your husband or the father of your child can gather it for you as mine did. It's a good way to test his supportiveness. Remember, though, it must be *fresh* dung. The best way to gather it is to wait behind a crocodile who is moving his or her bowels. When the dung emerges, thrust a skate board under the anus to catch it. Do *not* use plastic bags! Their crinkly sound tends to anger the crocodile."

"Is it possible to get the dung from zoos?" asked Polly.

Ms. Garrison-Talbot's eyes hardened. "The zoos have been totally unsupportive."

"What are the chances of setting up a meaningful dialogue with zoo directors?"

"Nonexistent," Ms. Garrison-Talbot said grimly. "We've tried to get our dung through the proper channels but we met with mockery at every turn. My car was even defaced. Someone wrote 'baby sitter' on the windshield and a *male* veterinarian referred to me as the 'ding-dung lady.' "

Polly Bradshaw grimaced in disgust. "We'll never be

free until they stop calling us ladies. Grace, what are your plans for the Birth Bucket League now?"

"Polly, we're going to fight for our rights to crocodile dung. We're setting up a letter-writing campaign to put pressure on the zoos, and my husband is chairing the Ad Hoc Dung Now committee from his hospital bed in Everglades Memorial. We're not going to give up until every woman is able to purchase crocodile dung from the zoo of her choice."

"Beautiful! Right on!" cheered Polly Bradshaw.

"In the meantime, I can recommend some substitutes for crocodile dung. Moldy bread is the best. Crumble it and line the bottom of your birth bucket with it. It's soft, and a natural source of penicillin, which means it's sterile. And best of all, it's easy to obtain—every active, involved woman's kitchen is full of it."

She turned the birth bucket on its rim and rolled it over to Polly Bradshaw.

"The League would like to present this to you in gratitude for your interest and your work in the Women's Liberation movement."

Polly received her gift with effusive thanks and signed off.

"That's all for now. Join us Monday when my guest will be Boudicca Vigilant, activist, revolutionary, and member of Women's International Terrorist Conspiracy from Hell, who will discuss her book, *Disarming Rapists: The Surgical Solution.*"

I turned off the TV and poured myself an even stiffer drink and brooded about the big publishing contracts feminists were getting. I wondered if I should try to climb on the Women's Lib bandwagon. First, I would have to change my name—Isabel Fairfax lacked the necessary agitprop crunch. I toyed with Zenobia Alert for a few minutes, and then gave up. I had nothing to say to a feminist readership. I hoped they *all* got raped by a battalion of Turkish cavalry. Not by the Turks—by the horses.

I sat drinking, too tired to bother with dinner. Sometime later, I heard my next door neighbor come home, and soon the dull thwacking sound started up. What was he, she, or it doing in there? I yawned, had yet another drink, and finally called it a day. Stripping down to pants and bra, I crawled into Gioppi's lumpy couch and fell asleep.

Sometime around midnight, I was blown out of bed by the explosion.

It started as a great gulping roar, like a Wagnerian treatment of the belching of the gods, and turned into a blast-off worthy of Cape Kennedy. Before I had time to be scared, I was on the floor in the middle of a pile of books.

When I got to my feet, the building was quivering. Outside, screaming people poured into the street and dogs barked all over the neighborhood. I stumbled through the book-strewn blackness and turned on the lights, which miraculously worked, and looked around.

The six hundred books I owned, which I had kept in neat piles all over the floor, were now in messy piles. But what really riveted my attention was the fiberboard wall that separated me from my next door neighbor. It was starting to take on all the elements of a Regency novel: a ripping noise like the heroine's bodice, a corner-to-corner slit like the villain's grin, a buckling like the old baronet's knees, and a waft of powder filling the air as though from a dowager's dusted bosom. And of course, since no Regency is complete without the collapse of an olde Englishe sea wall, the two-by-four studs snapped in half and Gioppi's chintzy room-divider gave up the ghost.

Now I no longer had to wonder who my next door

neighbor was. All I had to do was look into the other apartment. There, sprawled on the floor, wearing an *I Am a Human Being* nightshirt and clutching the birth bucket, was Polly Bradshaw.

We stared at each other in disbelief. For a brief moment I thought I had left the TV on. She was the last person I had seen before falling into bed half drunk; maybe I hadn't really gone to sleep; maybe I was still watching "Heated Topics."

Gradually my mind cleared and I remembered the *P. Bradshaw* next to my *I. Fairfax* on the mailboxes. I had noticed it when I moved in but it had not registered on me while I was watching her show. I was sure I had not met her in the hallway, but that wasn't unusual considering the weird hours I kept. Night people never meet anybody.

"I saw you on television," I said unoriginally. Why not? It's already replaced *E pluribus unum.*

"What happened?"

Hearing sirens, we pulled on our clothes and ran downstairs. The first person we saw was Gioppi in his V.F.W. cap, talking excitedly with a crowd of policemen. He hurried over when he saw me.

"I told you so! They was Weathermen, four of 'em, building bombs in my cellar! The dirty Commies blew theirselves up! How's that for starters?"

He was beside himself with joy. The decorations he had won in World War II were lined up on his lapel; the most prominent one was a Good Conduct medal with a spillover of oak-leaf clusters. He must have been the company brown nose.

Just then we heard a policeman identifying the dead Weathermen for a reporter. Naturally, their names were Farnham, Durham, Denham, and Bingham. *Eh, paesano!* Gioppi the Wasp-hater beamed.

A few minutes later, somebody from the coroner's office arrived and matters got ghoulish, to Gioppi's unbridled glee. The coroner's man happened to be Italian, too, so we were singled out for a real treat. He went into the smoking building and emerged momentarily with a container about the size of a dishpan, covered with heavy black plastic. He held it out to Gioppi like a thoughtful neighbor in time of need, saying, "I want you to have this."

"Farnham," he intoned, whereupon Gioppi lifted the cover and picked up a finger encircled by a Harvard class ring.

"I went to Boston College night school," Gioppi said proudly.

Over the next couple of hours, Farnham, Durham, Denham, and Bingham were found here and there in the shattered cellar of the house adjoining ours and in the back courtyards of both. Gioppi was like a child on an Easter egg hunt. Knowing that he would never again be in such a good mood, I followed him to the ambulance where he was turning in a foot and told him about our wall.

"What wall?"

He had grasped the situation perfectly. Polly and I took him upstairs and showed him the damage.

"When can you put up a new wall?" we demanded.

His eyes slid off to the side in that familiar Gioppi way. "Soon," he said.

"When?"

"Very soon. Just as soon as I see the insurance people."

"When are you going to see them?"

"Soon."

He beat a hasty retreat. Polly and I looked at each other and then at the mess. In the middle of the now-spacious room, lying half in my section and half in hers, was a Pat Nixon dartboard. That explained the thwacking sound.

We introduced ourselves formally, standing in the rubble exchanging pleasantries like two Londoners after a buzz-bomb attack. She asked me where I worked and seemed surprised by my answer.

"Didn't you hear the typewriter through the . . . wall?" She shook her head. "I've been doing volunteer work at the Self-Sufficiency Center every night for weeks. They need all the help they can get," she said gravely.

An uncomfortable silence fell, brought on by the discoveries we were making as we glanced into each other's apartment. There was an Angela Davis Defense Fund poster in her kitchen. While I contemplated that, her eyes locked onto my mantel, where I had hung the sampler I embroidered under Granny's tutelage:

> *God bless the squire and his relations*
> *And keep us in our proper stations*

She turned to me with an inscrutable expression. "Well, I guess we're going to be roommates for a few days."

"I guess we are." She was staring at my pile of *National Review*'s.

"Well," we said in unison.

We returned to our beds. Polly fell asleep right away but I lay awake thinking. Gioppi's ha-ha policy was probably with the Ha-Ha Insurance Company. He would never build a new wall, never. I was stuck in this Jericho with a Women's Libber for a roommate. It was almost as bad as sleeping with Ramsey Clark.

From *The Late George Apley:* "There are still a few bottles of Madeira in the cellar, though I am afraid the increasing motor traffic on Beacon Street has shaken them a bit."

2

To love her was a liberal education.

—Sir Richard Steele

The next day was Saturday. I assumed Polly would want to sleep late after the explosive happening but I was wrong. She was a morning person.

Shortly after sunrise I was awakened by something that sounded like a Gioppi drain fighting a losing battle against corrosion.

"Ushuum! Ushuum!"

I put one eye over the edge of the blanket and saw her. She was folded up on the floor in the lotus position with her fingers circled and her toes sticking out of her knees. I rolled over and went back to sleep. An hour later I was awakened again, this time by a *ta-click, ta-click-ta-click.* I surfaced again and found her exercising on a walking machine. It looked like a large scale with a revolving conveyor belt. With shoulders back and head held high, she was going purposefully nowhere.

The third time I woke up she was standing beside my bed with a mug of coffee.

"Are you planning to get up soon?" she asked reproachfully. "It's nine o'clock."

"Is it only ni—" My voice failed in mid-sentence. I reached for my cigarettes, lit one, and started hacking.

"Would you like some breakfast? I made a pot of oatmeal."

"Awwhhhrrr!"

"Are you all right? Here, I brought you some coffee. It's decaffeinated. Take a sip."

She glanced down disapprovingly at the overflowing ashtray and made several helpless gestures in my direction while I choked and gagged my way into a new day. At last I was able to breathe well enough to finish my cigarette. I sat up, face flushed and eyes streaming, and reached for the coffee.

"Thank you," I croaked.

Just then something large, orange, and alive crawled out from under her bed.

"Oh, there's Quadrupet. Last night scared him so much he went into hiding. I hope you don't mind cats."

Mind cats? My spirits rose. Feminist or not, she couldn't be too bad if she had a cat.

"I love cats," I said.

"Well, I hate them, but I can't get rid of him. He came in one day and refused to leave."

Quadrupet gave me a glance of heartwarming contempt and leaped up on my bed, planting himself just far enough away so that I had to stretch to pet him.

Polly fixed herself a cup of coffee and returned to my bedside. She looked around for an empty chair but all the chairs were piled with books. She gave up and perched on the bottom of the bed.

"Well!" she said with a bright smile. The unspoken words were *here we are.* "What kind of things do you write?"

I had a mouthful of coffee and smoke so I nodded my head at the pile of manuscript carbons on the table. She leaned over and read the title page and frowned.

"It's about a rake?"

"All my books are about rakes." I sighed. "I wanted to start with something simple while I was learning the mechanics of fiction. Someday I'll write about real people."

"They made us read something in school called 'The Man With a Hoe' but I think it was a poem."

We exchanged wary stares: two people in search of a wavelength. I drained the coffee and threw back the covers.

"I think I'll get dressed now."

When I emerged from the bathroom she was picking up pieces of the wall and stacking them neatly beside the door, arranging them according to size and degree of damage.

"For picket signs," she explained.

I felt like saying "It's my wall, too," but I didn't. When she had gotten all the pieces picked up, she started cutting the fiberboard into neat rectangles and tacking them onto the broken studs. While she was thus engaged I got my broom and dustcatcher and started sweeping up. It was a discouraging task; the fiber particles kept rising like strands of hemp from a hangman's rope after the drop.

When we had finished, Polly turned to me with another bright smile.

"Time for lunch."

It was ten-thirty. I had another cup of coffee and joined her at her table. I would have preferred to sit alone at mine but for some reason we couldn't seem to go our separate ways. We were caught up in the psychology of strangers brought together by a disaster.

She opened her refrigerator door and removed a pristine covered icebox jar. I had never seen such a neat, clean refrigerator. She had decanted her tomato juice into a covered pitcher decorated with little red pictures of ripe tomatoes. Mine was still in the can and decorated with two V-shaped indentations encrusted with brownish goo.

The icebox jar contained alfalfa weed. She emptied it onto a plate, sprinkled some lemon juice on it, and poured herself a glass of skim milk. She sat down and began to eat.

"Are you sure you won't have some alfalfa? It's delicious."

I smiled carefully and shook my head.

"How about a glass of milk?"

Awwhhhrrr! "No, thank you."

"You know, my Uncle Ezra writes. I wish you could meet him, but he lives in California now. Have you ever read any of his books?"

She got up and went to the tiny bookcase that Gioppi provided. I had one just like it. It was the size of a night table with two shelves. Polly's was as neat as her refrigerator; in fact, there were only three books in it. She brought them to the table and handed them to me.

They were written by Ezra Standish Bradshaw and bore the imprint of the Spartacus Press in Greenwich Village. The titles were:

Like It or Lump It: The Coming Social Change
Whales Are Human, Too
The Goading of America: A History of the Bradshaw Family

Recognition dawned—horribly. She was one of *those* Bradshaws. . . . I glanced warily at her as she chomped her way through the alfalfa patch. No wonder she was a feminist. Feminism was tame compared with some of the causes the Bradshaws took up. Leaders of Wasp America's loony left for more than two centuries, they ran to anarchistic Unitarian ministers, little old ladies given to missionary uplift, and derailed sociologists who roamed the ghettos telling the poor to sell their valuables and buy guns. Wherever you find a round hole, you'll find a Bradshaw sticking halfway out of it. The first sentence in *The Goading of America* summed them up: "Margaret

Fuller accepted the Universe but the Bradshaws do not."
I browsed through the book. It was full of family photos with captions like "Aunt Tabitha after her hunger
strike" and "Uncle Soames arrives in Harlan County."
Not surprisingly, there were a great many pictures of in-
jured people; the Bradshaws were happiest when they
were beating themselves into plowshares and losing fingers to mimeograph machines, pubic hair to hot tar, and
shoulders to the common weal. Their masochism resulted in very confusing captions, such as "Rev. Nathan (on
stretcher) being aided by wife Abigail (with bandage)
waving to Jared Bradshaw in departing police van (not
shown)." The only photos that did not need explanatory
cutlines were the ones taken at sit-down strikes in the
thirties: all the Bradshaws were standing up and making
speeches.

Polly was scooping up the last of her alfalfa. It looked
like green hair with nits.

"What are you going to do today?" she asked brightly.
Go back to bed. "Work."

"Well, I'll be out of your way. I'm going to picket a funeral parlor."

"A funeral parlor?"

"Yes. Have you seen their ad in the Yellow Pages?"
She fetched the book and opened it to the offending en-
try: "To Ease Your Mind, We Employ Female Attendants."

She put the directory back and took a picket sign from
the closet. It read: MISS GOODY TWO SHOES IS DEAD.

She waved at me with two fingers in a V-for-victory
sign and left. I crossed over to my own territory and
curled up on my bed beside Quadrupet. Soon we fell
asleep in each other's arms.

Since Polly had brought me my morning coffee and
offered me lunch, I felt I should cook dinner. When she

returned from the funeral parlor she sniffed the air appreciatively and gave me another bright smile.

"What're you cooking?"

"Something that's white and oval and crawls up your leg. Uncle Ben's perverted rice."

She frowned and shook her head. "You mean *con*verted," she corrected. "It's a process that puts back many of the nutrients that are lost when white rice is polished."

I dumped some stroganoff on top of my failed joke and we sat down at my table. I studied her as we ate. Aside from that touch of the games mistress that marks old-stock Yankee females, she was definitely what men called "too pretty to be a feminist." If you can imagine a strawberry blonde with Faye Dunaway cheekbones who picketed an undertaker, that was Polly in a Bradshaw nutshell.

After dinner I offered her coffee and brandy. It mellowed her and she began to talk about herself.

She had majored in economics at Radcliffe so she would be ready to redistribute the world's wealth when the revolution came. Meanwhile, she had worked briefly in the trust department of a bank—two weeks, to be exact—before being fired for circulating petitions demanding the abolition of inheritance rights, and free safety deposit boxes for poor women.

After that she had done some modeling. Most of her jobs had been glove ads—her fingers were almost as long as her legs—and she had done a brief stint as "Problem Elbow" in an ad for cream to make elbows smooth. The same firm wanted her to do "Freckles" but she had refused to countenance products that generated appearance anxiety in women.

Her Hammurabi-like instinct for laying down laws and her refusal to trade on her looks caused one uproar after another. The manufacturer of Boy Hip Jeans begged her to model his product but she would not work for him unless he also hired a woman whom Boy Hip Jeans would not fit. When he balked at that she produced an amputee, bringing forth cries of "meshuggeneh!" and a curse on her house.

Finally the model agency, used to girls who were willing to do anything to get work, gave her the boot and blacklisted her—worldwide, she added proudly. It was a Bradshaw first.

Her job on "Heated Topics" grew out of the publicity surrounding her citizen's arrest of a construction worker who whistled at her. She had marched onto the building site, put her hand on the worker's shoulder, and intoned, "Come with me." The worker, thinking, as he later explained, that she was a hot patooty, followed her all the way to the police station, where she cited an old colonial law still on the books that prohibited "sinfull and lustfull soundyngs." The case turned into such a brouhaha that the public television people offered her a half-hour afternoon talk show.

"It's important work because there's so much that needs to be done for women, but the pay is peanuts," she sighed.

That surprised me. I thought TV personalities made big money. I also thought the Bradshaws were rich. They had been once, back in the heyday of the Bradshaw Shipping Line. The early Bradshaws had been such a notorious pack of blackbirding, rum-running, penny-pinching Yankees that their guilt-ridden descendants had found it necessary to give all their money away to wild-eyed liberal causes. The only one left who was comfortably off was Uncle Ezra, who made a mint on the lecture circuit talking about saving the whales, an obsession with direct links to the New Bedford branch of the family.

"That's the story of my life," Polly finished. "Tell me about you."

I didn't think she was ready for it but she had enough brandy in her to remain vertical, so I began. When I was through she looked stunned, but there was a missionary gleam in her eye.

"You need to work out your prejudices," she said flatly.

"I don't have anything against the *Lusitania*, I just wouldn't want my sister to go down on it."

She frowned. "I thought you said you were an only child?"

Jesus. . . . The girl was unreal. I wondered if she had an *I Am a Humorless Feminist* nightshirt. I fixed another round of spiked coffee and the talk turned to men.

"How many lovers have you had?" she asked me.

I hesitated. Would she understand the writer's need to gather experience? "Ten," I replied.

Her hairline moved. "Ten! Are you sure?"

"A lady never loses count."

Now a gleam of grudging admiration joined the missionary gleam. "I've only had one," she confessed. "We lived together. Here, in fact," she added, waving into her section of the wreckage. "We had a viable relationship for a while but his openness was a token meetedness. He wasn't willing to make a serious commitment." A critical, puzzled note crept into her voice. "He wasn't serious about anything. He was always laughing. Something would happen that wasn't a bit funny, but he would double over and grab his stomach and laugh till the tears rolled down his cheeks." She shook her head. "He was really sick."

"When did you break up with him?"

"Four months ago. I came home one night and told him my consciousness-raising group was forming a masturbation workshop and he started that crazy laughing again. I got mad and told him I didn't see the humor in it at all, but that only made him laugh harder. We discussed him at my CR group and they said it was reactive hysteria triggered by a perceived threat from my clitoris."

"Did he name Quadrupet?" I asked.

She blinked in surprise. "Why, yes. How did you know?"

"Just a hunch."

The next day, Polly came up with her plan.

"How would you like to institute an open communal environment based on mutual cooperation?"

"You mean live together?"

"Yes! You know Gioppi. He'll never get around to building a new wall. If we rented this place as one apartment we could save money, yet we'd both still have the same space we had before."

She waited for my response with a curiously bright expression of restrained eagerness that I recognized as the Bradshaw missionary gleam, the same look that shone forth from the photos in Uncle Ezra's family history. She was talking thrift but her genes were crying out for a captive audience of the unenlightened, and I was the most unenlightened person she had ever met. She had sighted her Moby-Dick and it was me.

I didn't want to live with anybody, least of all a Women's Libber, but I did want to gather experience. I remembered the resentful envy I felt whenever another feminist writer became a literary lion. Books about feminism *were* hot. Maybe if I lived with Polly I would be able to write one, too, and get in on the best-seller gravy train. After all, she had an ulterior motive for wanting to live together; why couldn't I have one?

"Okay," I said.

"Wonderful! Let's go find Gioppi."

We did not have to look far. He had returned early to help the police look for stray bits of Farnham, Denham,

Durham, and Bingham. We found him in the back area-
way posing beside a pile of blasting caps and doorbell
wire for a photographer from *The Italo-American News.* He
was still wearing his V.F.W. cap, to which he now added
a snappy salute.

With great reluctance he came upstairs with us. Polly
went to her files and extracted a copy of the Tenants'
Rights Code. She shoved it under his nose and spoke in
her chowdery twang.

"One ap*ah*tment, one rent."

"It ain't one apartment, it's two! You got two kitchens
and two bathrooms, right? And two doors!"

"And no wall. One ap*ah*tment, one rent."

Gioppi's eyes slid off to the side in their usual fashion
and came to rest on my stenotype machine. It had a startling effect on him. With his history of criminal negli-
gence he had probably seen a lot of them. They say a
returning jury will not look at a defendant if they have
voted him guilty, but court reporters have even better
clues to go by. Perjurers always stare at the stenotype
machine the way Gioppi was staring at mine now. He
probably thought we had a lawyer in the closet ready to
take a deposition.

"One ap*ah*tment, one rent," Polly repeated.

I looked at her curiously. Gone for the moment was
the idealistic uplifter of humanity. She had turned into
the very spit of old Cap'n Nehemiah, the lipless wonder
of rapacity who founded the Bradshaw Shipping Line.
Gioppi saw it, too, and gave in.

The open communal environment based on mutual cooperation was now underway.

Boiled down, our new arrangement meant that Quadrupet now sprayed my apartment as well as hers, but
Polly never boiled anything down. The first thing she
did was make a seven-page list of household chores,

called AREAS OF RESPONSIBILITY, that left nothing to chance. Everything was set up like a class schedule; MWF for this, TTh for that, and something else on SSun. FT meant "free time" and there was very little of it.

It was my first experience with an anal-retentive personality. She could not seem to do anything without first checking her list, and each time she went over it she reworked the dots after the numbers, circling, pressing, and stabbing at them with her pencil until the back of the paper was full of black-bordered holes. She made two copies of it and taped one on each icebox. What it actually said was very simple: I would do the cooking, Polly would do the dishes, and we would shop for groceries together.

When you cook for someone else, you make a special effort. When you are a Southerner imbued with a tradition of gracious hospitality, you put yourself out even more. I cooked up a storm: cornbread, smothered chicken, spoon bread, fried apples, hush puppies, and barbecued ribs. Polly gobbled everything and didn't gain an ounce; I gobbled everything and swelled up like a balloon. By the end of our first six weeks together, I looked like her politics and she looked like mine.

Housekeeping was declared an individual responsibility; each of us cleaned what used to be our respective apartments. The line of demarcation was the scarred area of the floor where the wall studs had stood. Given Polly's literal mind, I shouldn't have been so stunned when, finding a piece of discarded manuscript that had drifted across the border, she bent down, tore off her half, and let my half lie there. It stayed there for two weeks because Southern standards of housekeeping had changed drastically after the Emancipation Proclamation. The only thing in my apartment that wasn't dusty was the bourbon bottle.

Polly, on the other hand, was Ms. Clean. Though she

scorned the concept of housework as an instrument of woman's oppression, her section of our domain could have passed a white-glove inspection. It sounds like some sort of unresolved conflict but it wasn't. There was a very simple reason behind it. Like every spit-and-polish housekeeper since the dawn of civilization, she did not like to read.

Mentally, she was what employers in pre-Lib days dared to call a "sharp gal," the kind they had in mind when they wrote that classic ad: "Seek bright, quick, self-starting miss desiring opportunity for advancement. Must be good at detail."

In common with most math majors she had an astronomical I.Q. but her pool of general culture was Dismal Swamp. Like the magazine editor who wrote "Who he?" in the margin next to "Andromeda," she gloried in militant ignorance.

"Gordian knot? Never heard of it. Needlework is a male conspiracy to keep women passive."

"Mary McCarthy? Never heard of her. You must mean Bernadette Devlin."

"Stonehenge? Never heard of one. Better call a locksmith."

As the list of never-heard-of-its got longer and longer, the temptation to pull her leg became irresistible. I lay in wait for the perfect chance and she handed it to me on a platter.

She belonged to a group called "Feminist Consumers United Against Brand Names," whose members had taken a solemn oath to buy only generic items and report suspicious or recalcitrant retailers to the group's watchdog committee.

Knowing that I had studied Latin, one night she asked me if I knew the generic name for a certain laxative suppository.

"Ultima Thule," I replied.

She didn't bat an eye. Opening her memo book to U, she handed it to me and asked me to write it down. I complied and she left for the drugstore. Half an hour later she returned wearing a smile of grim triumph.

"He said he never heard of it. That proves he's part of the pharmaceutical companies' conspiracy."

She filed a watchdog report. Shortly thereafter the newsletter of the FCUABN came out with banner headlines about the mysterious unavailability of Ultima Thule suppositories. "They've even taken it out of the pharmacopoeia!" wailed the editorial, and issued a call for the usual flood of protest letters to the Food and Drug Administration.

I had struck a blow for liberal arts. I struck another one a week later when I convinced her that every feminist should read *Madame Bovary.* I gave her my copy and waited. And waited. She consigned it to FT, so it took her forever to get through it. She finally finished it one night while I was cooking dinner. I held my breath as she came into the kitchen.

"What did you think of it?" I asked eagerly.

"She needed credit counseling."

I gave up striking blows for liberal arts.

As I got to know her better, I realized that her political stance was rooted in something even deeper than her Bradshaw genes. Like most female reformers, she had a feminine nature and a masculine mind, a fatal blend that produces a knight in petticoats, determined to rescue humanity in distress and carry it off across a sidesaddle. Polly's motivating force was love; she wanted a world in which everybody loved everybody else whether they liked it or not, but she set this overflowing feminine cup in motion with a thoroughly masculine arsenal of charts, graphs, quorums, task forces, ad hocs, tunnel vision, and lists.

Her fondest dream was of finding pathetic creatures in desperate need of her help, which was why she hated cats. She was constantly looking around for a worthy cause, and since our new free-form apartment was still small, every time she looked around she saw me.

With the subtlety of a child yelling "Tag, you're it!" she set out to improve my health. Her first assault consisted of taping the "Seven Deadly Signs of Cancer" on my bathroom mirror and delivering a daily lecture on the perils of tobacco during my morning hacking sessions.

"Lung cancer is an equal opportunity disease. Back when smoking was considered unladylike, women didn't get it, which led people to think that it was a man's disease from which women were naturally immune. But now," she said ominously, "women are catching up."

"Awwhhhrrr!"

"It's not *logical* to go on smoking when you *know* it's dangerous. Look, it's right here on the package. Listen. 'Warning: The Surgeon General has determined that cigarette smoking is dangerous to your health.' They've made *studies* on this. The Surgeon General wants to *help* you!"

"The federal government has three duties. Print the money, deliver the mail, and declare war. Give me my cigarettes."

"If you won't get the smoke out of your lungs, at least you could get some fresh air into them. Let's start a jogging program! You never go out. You stay up half the night and then sleep through the most healthful part of the day. Every morning when I do my exercises I have to look at you lying in bed."

"Why do you do all those exercises? You weigh less than me and you're seven inches taller."

"Do you think you need a metabolism test?" she asked hopefully. "The Artemis Clinic for Women has just opened and—"

"I've already had a metabolism test."

"What did it measure?"

"Lizard."

Convinced that women could do anything men could do, she rejected the notion that menstruation is a hindrance, so the first time she found me hunched over the john vomiting she jumped to conclusions.

"Why didn't you tell me? I'll call the Center. You might have to go out of state but don't worry, I'll take care of it. Suction is better than curettage. It's just like vacuuming the floor. Whoosh, and it's all over. I went to a suction seminar and they showed movies. There's nothing to it, just *whoosh!* You can go home the same day and they give you free orange juice."

"UrrrrrrAAGGGH!"

"I've got the forms. Do you want me to fill them out for you? It's the first trimester, isn't it? Count. You've got to count. Think back. Try to remember when it happened. Do you want to have it and put it up for adoption or do you want to keep it? Just tell me what you want to do; I've got forms for everything. I've also got some brochures that explain everything legalwise. If you want, you can pick out the adoptive parents now and go live with them. It's a new alternative choice called 'Mom Times Two.' The adoptive mother pretends that you're her sister. When the baby arrives she thinks she's its aunt. If she isn't convinced, they'll send somebody around to hypnotize her. Do you want me to call them? They've got a list of women with liberated husbands. Would you like to talk to a counselor? I know everybody there. I've also got some pamphlets on—my God! You're bleeding!"

"Of course I'm bleeding! I've got the curse!"

She shrank back and leaned against the basin. I rested my clammy cheek on the toilet seat and we contemplated each other.

"The curse?"

"Yes, you know—that wonderful thing that happens every month."

I reached a shaking hand into the cabinet and took out a Kotex. Polly left and I fixed myself up and hobbled back to bed with my heating pad. She was waiting for me, full of sisterly solicitude.

"Would you like some milk?"

I almost threw up again. "No, some bourbon, if you please."

She brought me a drink and sat down beside the bed. "I've never seen anyone suffer so much," she said.

"It runs in the family."

"Don't say that! That's an obsolete notion."

"It is not. Granny had cramps, Mama had them, and Aunt Edna still has them. It's the Upton womb."

"The what?"

"Upton was Granny's maiden name. Every doctor in Virginia knows about the Upton womb. Granny's grandmother's doctor gave a speech on it to the state A.M.A. meeting way back when. He called it the Gettysburg of womankind. Everything that can go wrong with a womb has gone wrong with one of ours."

"You mean they actually call it the Upton womb?" she asked incredulously.

"Of course. Granny's is in a jar at University of Virginia medical school. She donated it when she had her hysterectomy. They needed it to study because there're Uptons all over the state. We were First Families so it's had time to spread."

"The male-dominated medical profession has conspired for centuries to convince us that we're weak. Your grandmother," she said darkly, "was brainwashed."

"That's like saying a K.G.B. psychiatrist is brainwashed."

"I have an idea," she said brightly. "Why don't you

attend the Dysmenorrhea Summer Camp? I had the
founder on my show a few months ago. It's a new treatment combining physical therapy, psychological counseling, and group supportiveness. It's up in Maine. You
could borrow my car and—"

"I can't drive."

She regarded me with a look of pure horror. I could
have bitten off my tongue; it was something I had been
planning to keep from her.

"Why not?" she demanded.

I hesitated, loath to tell such a ruthless humanitarian
that I was an agoraphobiac. Her old kit bag was packed
with centers and clinics for every known affliction ending in *iac* and she would like nothing better than a chance
to carry me to one in her arms, explaining to the curious
along the way, "She's not heavy, she's my sister." She
would also want to have a "dialogue" on Origins of Your
Agoraphobia, which would mean another bout with her
literal-mindedness. I had never gotten lost as a child—
nobody could get lost in Queen Caroline—but she would
insist that I was burying a trauma. She would never understand that agoraphobia was my quirky armor against
a gregarious America, and a tool that had helped me to
acquire the inner resources and private space she wanted
for all women. But there was no use trying to explain
this to her. Like all reformers, she stood four-square behind individuality because it was the best position from
which to give individuals a good hard shove.

I cast around for an excuse she would swallow.

"A girl reaches driver's-license age at the same time
she starts to date," I said nonchalantly. "Her boyfriends
drive her wherever she wants to go, so she puts off learning."

"I dated when I was sixteen but I had a driver's license," she countered.

"Queen Caroline is such a small town I could walk
wherever I needed to go."

"A small town in the middle of *nowhere.*"

She was starting to get suspicious. I got desperate.

"Cars pollute the environment," I said loftily.

"You hate the environment. You've been anti-earth ever since Ayn Rand came out in favor of factory smoke. As soon as you're over your period I'm going to teach you how to drive."

"What?"

It was a rhetorical question but that never bothers a Bradshaw. "I'm going to teach you how to drive."

"But I don't want to learn!"

"Yes, you do, and you're going to," said the liberal.

3

It is not true that woman was made from man's rib. She was made from his funny bone.

— Sir James Barrie

The driving project started out auspiciously enough when I got a score of one hundred on the written test for the learner's permit. Polly the Helper broke out in I-told-you-so optimism but I knew it meant nothing. I was a test-taker, that's all. In college I knew that *Sartre* went with *existentialism* and now I knew that *octagon* went with stop sign. I hoped I wouldn't hit one, as Aunt Edna did when she took her driving test. Her argument was "Well, I stopped, didn't I?" when the examiner flunked her, as though driving *over* a stop sign were the real sin. It was one of many things that haunted me the first day Polly took me out on the road. Maybe this, too, ran in the family.

She had a Karmann Ghia that she kept in the underground parking garage at the TV studio. I looked at it dubiously. It had a stick shift. I knew about gears; I had shifted them for my high-school boyfriend so he wouldn't have to take his hand out of my blouse, but his

car had been an ancient one with the stick on the steering column. Polly's gear stick was on the floor, enclosed
in a little leather bag like a Victorian piano leg in panta-
lettes, so what little knowledge I had was useless.

She drove us out to Quincy, which she called "Quin-
zy," and stopped on a quiet residential street. I slipped
reluctantly into the driver's seat while she went round to
the trunk and took out the sign she had made from a
piece of our former wall: CAUTION! SUDDEN STOPS! She taped
it on the back of the car and got in beside me.

"Now," she began officiously, "assume the proper
driving posture. Both hands on the wheel at two o'clock
and ten o'clock and seat belt fastened."

I put both hands on the wheel and then removed them
to struggle with the seat belt. There were two, one for
the lap and another for across the shoulder. It was like
wrapping a mummy. I let go of the wrong piece at the
wrong time and hit myself on the nose with the buckle.
Polly reached over to do me up and poked me in the ribs.
I squealed and went into hysterics from stored-up fright,
but she saw nothing funny about assuming the proper
driving posture.

She finally finished fixing the belts. "You are now
ready to drive," she intoned.

I stretched out my feet but they touched nothing except warm air.

"You have to adjust the seat to your height," she said.
"The lever's under the front cushion."

"I can't bend over, the belts are too tight."

She reached behind my legs and pulled. I shot forward
against the wheel like a cannonball. The shoulder belt
snapped open and covered my left eye like a pirate's
patch.

"You are now ready to drive," she said again.

"Oh, yeah?"

She turned and looked at me critically. Then, without

cracking a smile: "That's a hazard. Your vision must be unimpeded at all times."

I glared at her with my remaining eye while she readjusted the belt. This time it was too tight.

"Let me take off the top one," I pleaded. "I feel like I'm suffocating."

"It never bothers me."

I refrained from pointing out that she was virtually titless. We argued for a few minutes and finally she gave in and let me wear the lap belt only. I was now ready to drive.

I turned the key and the engine roared into life. Instinctively, I jumped back but went nowhere. At Polly's instruction, I "depressed" the clutch and then concentrated on finding first gear. I found it at last and shifted.

"Now, lift your left foot as you depress your right one on the gas pedal. Gradually! If you do it too fast you'll—"

All sorts of red lights went on and the motor stopped. It happened three more times.

"Why does it keep stalling?" I wailed.

"Because you take your foot off the clutch too fast! Give it a little gas and raise your foot slowly until you feel it engage. Try it again. Feel that little click? That means you've engaged. It's like sex—you have to wait for the exact right moment."

That made me wild, since I had long harbored the suspicion that she was not very good in bed. Now, covered with sweat and shaking all over, I exploded.

"I know how to have an orgasm! What I don't know is how to shift these goddamn gears!"

"Prudence Patience puts up pickles," she singsonged.

In my mind's eye I saw her skinny ancestors in their little white caps, working from dawn to dusk. I wished one of them were in front of me now.

Finally, I managed to proceed down the street in first without stalling. Polly cheered me on.

"Beautiful! Now clutch and shift to second."

"What's that awful noise?"

"Take your foot off the gas!"

"It'll stop going if I do!"

"No, it won't. You can't depress the clutch and the gas at the same time. That's called revving the motor."

"What? I can't hear you!"

"Revving the motor! You're doing it again!"

Two days later, she decided I was good enough to leave the residential areas and take to the traffic. It was in the business district of Quincy that I had my first encounter with a four-way stop. Nothing could have been more calculated to bring out our respective political personalities. I considered it a democratic horror, but it was the sort of thing that filled Polly with gulpy we-the-people emotion.

"You take turns," she said happily. "Whoever gets to the intersection first goes first. It's voluntary self-policing."

"That's putting too much trust in human nature," I said darkly. "They ought to have a regular light. It's the only way to *make* people do the right thing."

I was scared to death. I knew *I* would wait my turn, but what about those other drivers? They might not have my internal gyroscope. I lurked at the stop sign and hunched over the wheel, scrutinizing their faces for some indication of their inner worth. The one on my left especially worried me: he had a weak chin.

Just then a chorus of horns sounded.

"Go on!" Polly yelled.

Five days later, she decided I was ready to take my road test.

"I hope you get a woman examiner," she said as she drove me to the Department of Motor Vehicles. We pulled into the test area and waited. A few minutes later, the office door opened. Polly looked up expectantly; then her face fell.

"Oh, shit, it's a man."

"Suppose he says something about my wearing just the lap part of the belt?"

"Don't worry," she said with a crafty wink. "I'll handle it."

Oh-shit-it's-a-man was clearly an Irishman, weighted down with a neck full of religious medals on a chain. The most prominent one, bigger than a silver dollar, featured St. Christopher. When he leaned down and stuck his head in the car window, the medal spun around and I saw the message on the flip side: *I am a Catholic. In case of accident, please call a priest.* I took it personally and started to shake.

He asked me to do the hand signals, then looked dubiously at my seat belt arrangement. "Your shoulder belt is unfastened," he chided.

"There's a medical reason for it," Polly piped up. "She's had a vasectomy."

I closed my eyes and put my head on the wheel. Ms. Malaprop rides again. . . .

Naturally she started babbling. "I mean mastectomy! I always get them confused. It was performed only two weeks ago so she's still sore. The doctor told her under no condition should she use the shoulder strap until everything heals up or else she'll rub a blister."

"All right, all right," said the examiner, holding up his hand in a placatory gesture.

As he got in beside me, he could not resist a furtive glance at my bosom. It was the same kind of look children used to give pregnant women back when pregnancy meant you had done something dirty. The glance, his medals, and Polly's blooper unnerved me so much that I flunked the road test.

Twenty horrible minutes later, we were back. Polly's

hopeful face fell when I gave her the thumbs-down signal. She listened while the examiner analyzed my performance.

"Due to deductions, you failed to qualify," he said in toneless, training-manual fashion. "You lost ten points for passing a school bus, five for driving over a fire hose, five for wide backing, five for driving on the sidewalk, five for joining a funeral procession—"

"I turned on my lights."

"We don't give credit for that. Let's see," he went on, continuing down his list. He frowned and gave a puzzled grunt. "This is something I've never come across before. I guess I'll call it 'inventing a new traffic law.' "

"What?" Polly said incredulously.

"She yielded the right of way to an Animal Rescue League truck."

"It reminded me of Quadrupet," I explained. She rolled her eyes.

The examiner went on. "And then we have turning into the wrong lane, driving in the bus lane, driving over an island, jerky stops, and failing to signal."

He totted up his figures and handed me the card. "Your score is two."

"Two?"

"That is correct."

"What did I get that for?"

"Your right turns. They were absolutely perfect." He shook his head. "I can't understand it."

"I can," said Polly.

He walked back to his office making the sign of the cross. I unhooked the seat belt and moved over and Polly got behind the wheel.

"See?" I said in exhausted triumph. "I told you I couldn't drive."

"If at first you don't succeed, try, try again."

"Please close the copybook."

She frowned pensively and looked around in confusion. "Did he leave something?"

"Jesus. . . ."

Although I done everything except break a wheel on a butterfly, Polly would not let me give up. The next morning, she literally dragged me out of bed and took me out on the roads again. We spent the entire session backing around the same corner while she held the door open to check my distance from the curb. Worse, she brought along her carpenter's folding rule to measure it. It was one of the items from her self-sufficiency tool box. She persisted in calling it a "folding carpenter's rule" and I just as persistently pointed out that it was the rule that folded, not the carpenter, but she was too saturated in Femspeak to hear the difference.

After I learned how to make my tires hug the curb, she cured me of my love affair with the brake by making me downshift to second when approaching an intersection and coast to a smooth stop. To test this, she brought along a huge picnic jug of grape juice and poured herself a brimful cup each time she saw a red light coming up. The idea was for me to stop so smoothly that she would not spill a drop.

To me, "not a drop" was a figure of speech. To Polly, it meant *not a drop.*

"Look," she said reproachfully, after she had consumed some seventeen cups. She pointed to a small purple stain on her pants leg. It was one drop.

"Don't you have to pee?" I asked nastily.

She frowned pensively. "No, do you?"

"Jesus. . . ."

She broke my habit of using the clutch as a footrest by yelling "FOOT!" at the top of her lungs whenever I did it. Once, a cop heard her and offered to give us an escort to a hospital where, he said earnestly, they had a bilingual emergency team.

Thanks to her rock-headed persistence, the next time I took my road test I passed with flying colors. To celebrate, I treated Polly to a seafood dinner in Lynn. I couldn't believe I had a driver's license at last; all through dinner I kept taking it out and looking at it. Polly kept telling me that I was now completely independent, but she said it without her usual feminist intensity, so for the first time, we thoroughly enjoyed each other's company.

Afterward, we walked along the shorefront and bought some clams to take home. It had been a perfect day, so of course it couldn't last. Something about the combination of Polly and me seemed to inspire Fate to surpass herself.

When we came to the dumpy part of the beach, we found an abandoned cement mixer lying on the sand. Childlike, we peered into the ball, but instead of the nothing we expected, we found the something nobody ever expects: a dead body.

It was a white female, approximately twenty-five years old. My fingers automatically tapped out the familiar words on an imaginary stenotype machine. Polly misinterpreted my gesture.

"Stay calm. You must stay calm; otherwise the newspapers will say 'the hysterical women who discovered the body.' They always say that, just like they always say 'the women passengers screamed' when they write about a skyjacking. Do some breathing exercises and then we'll go for the police. Ready? And one, and two, and thr—"

We both screamed. The corpse had moved.

As we clutched each other and backed away, the woman stuck her head out over the lip of the cement mixer and inched forward in a wormlike motion, but the effort was too much for her. Her head lolled and her arms fell out of the ball and dangled over the sand. Their color hinted at an interrupted embalming.

"She needs help!" Polly cried.

We pulled her out of her lair and tried to stand her on her feet but she kept buckling. She had Radical hair, long, frizzy, and dirty blond under a Navy surplus bosun's cap. That much was par for the course around Boston, but the rest of her would have attracted attention even on Beacon Hill.

She wore a green Marine Corps T-shirt tucked into an Army surplus canvas money belt, and a skirt made from an old pair of draperies that fastened to the money belt by the drapery hooks, which she had apparently never bothered to remove. I imagined her ripping them from someone's window like a hippie Scarlett O'Hara and fashioning a skirt on the spot. They must have been the floor-to-ceiling kind originally; the hem she had fixed up with safety pins of varying sizes and colors was a good ten inches deep. Under it peeked a pair of green rubber mud-boots with bright yellow lacing.

Whoever she was, she was not That Cosmo Girl; her witchiness was the kind that went with the eye of a newt. She looked like a necromancer gone wrong.

Polly tried slapping her lightly to bring her out of her funk. As she swayed to and fro, the marijuana fumes she gave off almost turned us on, too. At last her eyes opened and she gave us a zonked smile.

"What are you doing here?" Polly asked.

"I am here . . . I don't know."

"Where do you come from?"

"Many places."

It sounded like *Pelléas and Mélisande*. There was some more in the same collapsed vein before we finally got a complete sentence out of her.

"My thing is urban despair," she mumbled, then passed out again.

Polly turned to me, aglow with sisterly zeal. "We've got to help her! Let's take her home with us."

I gave her a wild look and opened my mouth to protest, then stopped. On any other day I could have objected, but not this one. I felt my new driver's license burning inside my wallet like a saint's stigmata. I didn't have the nerve to argue against her sisterhood support system after having just benefited from it myself.

Polly put her arm around the girl's waist. "See if she left anything in the cement mixer," she said. It was the sort of sentence I had never expected to hear.

I peered into the ball, certain I would find a pile of picked bones and a bowl of blood, but there was nothing except the usual Army surplus duffel bag painted with peace symbols. When I picked it up, it gave off a muffled twanging sound, so I figured she owned the usual guitar.

"Hold up her other side," Polly instructed. "We'll carry her between us."

Given the difference in our heights, it didn't work, so I went and got the car.

"Where'll we put her?" I said, looking at the tiny sports car in consternation. The back seat was a mere slit.

"I'll hold her in my lap," Polly said fervently.

I dumped the duffel bag in the slit and got behind the wheel. Polly slid in beside me and dragged our unconscious sister on top of her. I wondered if she would indulge her seat-belt compulsion at a time like this. Yes, she would; anal-retentives never give up. While I waited in gear, she pulled and stretched and buckled and clicked until the two of them were trussed and ready to drive. I wanted to buy the car from her just for the pleasure of taking a razor to those goddamn belts.

We headed back to Boston like Franz Josef's flunkies transporting the decomposing corpse of Marie Vetsera from Mayerling. Polly was making comforting sounds and cradling the girl's head.

"For God's sake, stop hugging her, Polly. You don't know what she might have."

"Urban despair! Urban despair!"

"I know . . . I know," Polly crooned.

"*Tant pis,*" I muttered.

Gioppi was fortunately nowhere in sight when we got to the house. I carried the duffel bag and the clams and pushed from behind, while Polly pulled from the front. In this manner we finally got Urban Despair up to our door.

The moment Quadrupet saw her he laid his ears back so far he looked like a weasel. We put her in a chair and Polly started flying around like a ministering angel fetching water and spirits of ammonia. I went through the duffel bag.

My first surprise was the musical instrument. It wasn't a guitar but a lute. I put it aside and reached into the bag again. This time I found something that contained her name. It was a dog-eared music manuscript.

" 'A Madrigal on the Death of Edward the Second,' " I read aloud. " 'An original composition by Gloria Hammond.' " Gioppi would love that; another no-good dirty Wasp.

The rest of her belongings consisted of a few extra pairs of underpants, a ratty fur jacket that looked like Good Will Surplus, and an electric curling iron. I couldn't imagine why she bothered to curl her hair considering what she looked like from the neck down. I put it down to that vestigial female vanity found in bag ladies who carry a sliver of mirror in their ragged pockets.

Polly glanced at the musical composition. "Edward the Second? Never heard of him. I wonder if I can get her to eat something? Give me one of those clams."

I reached into the bag and pulled out a fried clam. She put it in Gloria's mouth but it just lay there like an extra tongue. She took it out and threw it away.

"Maybe she's a diabetic," Polly said with alarm. "This could be a coma. Look, there's something in her money belt that feels like a medicine bottle! Maybe it's her insulin."

The money belt yielded plenty of medicine bottles but none of them contained insulin—just uppers and downers and lots of sugar cubes.

"She's a dope fiend!"

"Narcotics addict," Polly corrected. "What she needs is a good night's sleep." She started turning down her bed.

"Where are you going to sleep?" I asked.

"On the floor. I'll use the bolsters."

"Why don't you put her on the floor? She wouldn't know the difference. Why do you have to give your bed away?"

"Because she needs it more than I do."

"We don't know who she is or what she might do! She might get up in the middle of the night and find a knife and stab us while we're asleep!"

"That's a chance we'll have to take."

I poured myself a double bourbon and coaxed Quadrupet out from under the stove. I put him in my lap and we brooded together while Polly sat beside the snoring Gloria applying cold cloths.

When it was time for bed, she put the bolsters on the floor and tried to make a mattress out of them but it was an impossible task: they were wedges. Whichever way she turned them she ended up with geometric lumps. Mine were the same kind so there was only one thing to do.

"For God's sake, sleep with me," I grumbled.

The day beds Gioppi supplied were less than twin size. Polly fell asleep right away but I lay there trying to avoid her sharp bones; it was like being pressed in the Iron Maiden. Quadrupet slunk back under the stove and I was left alone with my thoughts.

Dear Prudence Patience:
I'm living with this nut and now she's brought home
another nut. I have a feeling that the new one is going
to be the Nut Who Came to Dinner. What shall I do?
Call Me Isabel

Dear Call:
It's obvious from your letter that you harbor élitist
attitudes. You must work on your prejudices. Remember
that the only bad people are cigarette-smokers.
Prudence Patience

That settled it. I decided to move out and leave Polly
to her strays. I would tell her tomorrow—if tomorrow
ever came.

It came. Polly got up first, bright and chipper and aching
to do good. I heard her bustling around in her kitchen
making coffee. She brought me a cup.
"Gloria's awake," she said happily. "Come in and see
her. She looks so much better."
I went solely out of curiosity. She was sitting up in
bed, still wearing her bosun's cap. To the eye of a Non-
Helper, she looked worse.
"Gloria, would you like some apple juice?" Polly
asked. "It's unfiltered."
"Yump."
She was too weak to hold the glass so Polly put it on
the night table and Gloria leaned over and slurped at it.
"Would you like a natural egg?"
"Nmmph."
When the apple juice had sunk below slurping level,
the Great Humanitarian held the glass to Gloria's lips
and helped her drain it. She smacked her mouth appreciatively
and asked for another. Polly ran and got it.
When she had drunk off the second one she looked al-

most normal except for the green rubber boots sticking
out of the sheets.

"You were really thirsty, weren't you?" Polly said
happily. "Now I'll get you some cof—"

"Whan that Aprille with his shoures soote/The
droghte of March hath percéd to the roote."

"Oh, my God, she's hallucinating!" Polly cried.

"No, she isn't. That's *The Canterbury Tales.*"

Even Polly had heard of them. We stood there, she in
alarm and I in growing empathy as Gloria went through
the entire Prologue without missing a beat. By the time
she finished I had revised my moving plans. Here was
somebody even more deeply mired in irrelevancy than I
was. She had struck such a blow for liberal arts that Polly was staggering.

Gloria got out of bed, went into the bathroom to
splash a little water on her face, and joined us at the table
for coffee. Except for looking a little blurry around the
edges, she was completely recovered.

"I'm a medievalist," she explained. "There was no urban despair in the Middle Ages. It was pre-Renaissance,
pre-industrial, pre-everything."

We had a Henry Adams in the house. "Did you major
in history?" I asked.

"Yes, but I'm really a medieval music historian. I did
my thesis on balladry in the reign of Edward the Second.
I set his murder to music."

"Who is Edward the Second?" Polly asked.

"King of England 1307–1327," Gloria replied with authority. "He was forced to abdicate by the Welsh barons.
They wanted to kill him but they had to find a way to do
it without leaving any marks of violence on his body so
they could pass it off as a natural death. How," she asked
rhetorically, "could they do it? Starvation was out, and
so were stabbing, poisoning, drowning, smothering, de-
fenestration, and exsanguination."

Polly jumped as though she had been electrocuted. "What are those last two?"

"Throwing him out of a window and draining off his blood."

"Oh."

"Finally, they figured out a way to do it that would leave no trace." She paused dramatically. "And since he was gay, it was also a symbolic punishment." She leaned forward, surveying us under beetle brows. "Do you know what they did to him?"

"No," I lied. "What?"

"They shoved a hollow reed up his ass, inserted a red-hot poker, and then withdrew the reed."

Polly emitted a squealy grunt and raised her bottom off the chair. It had hit her where she lived.

"No trace of foul play appeared on the person of the king," Gloria went on. "The deed wasn't discovered until the embalmer cut the body open to prepare it for burial and saw that there was no work to be done."

Polly listed further to starboard until she was perched on one hip. I saw her reach behind and give herself a surreptitious scratch. She hastened to change the subject.

"Wouldn't you like to take a shower, Gloria? And get into some clean clothes? We'll lend you something."

Gloria acquiesced with a blurry smile and went into Polly's bathroom. The Sister of Us All heaved a quavery sigh and changed hips, but her respite was short-lived. The water came on and Gloria started to sing one of her original compositions, called, we learned later, "Poore Ned's Burnyng Bunghole."

> *The royale arse did scorch and melte*
> *Where once Piers Gaveston's pryck was felte*
> *Where Hugh De Spenser plunged his rod*
> *And shot full wyll his manly wad*
> *Was rendered down to fiery suet puddying!*

"Oh, God," Polly groaned, flexing her fingers, "I can't make a fist!"

I drank black coffee and said nothing. It was one of the happiest moments of my life. A little later, the water shut off and Gloria emerged from the bathroom sans robe, sans towel, sans everything. She wasn't even wearing pubic hair. Her pudenda had been shaved as bald as an egg and painted with that garish antiseptic poetically known as gentian violet. Polly went all compassionate when she saw it; to her it was the mark of the free clinic. Having labored in different vineyards, all I could think of was *I never saw a purple twat and never hoped to see one.*

I drew the blinds and Polly produced a supportive smile and some fresh underwear. We breakfasted on scrambled eggs and cornbread. As we ate, Gloria told us how she had come to be in the cement mixer. She had lost her job as music teacher at an experimental private school a week before. The post had included faculty housing in addition to salary, and so, finding herself homeless as well as unemployed, she had decided to camp out on the beach with some radicals she knew. But the radicals had stolen her severance pay and, apparently, dumped her in the cement mixer when they mistook her bad drug trip for death. Or maybe she had climbed into the cement mixer by herself. She really couldn't say.

"I was fired for unconventional teaching methods," she confessed.

"If you were a man, they'd have called them 'innovative,' " Polly said darkly. "I'll help you file a discrimination suit!" She went to her file cabinet and took out a folder full of forms. "Now," she said, all businesslike, "tell me exactly what happened."

Gloria wiped her mouth on the back of her hand, medieval style. "I was telling my class about the Black Plague in the fourteenth century. I wanted to make it come alive for them, so I decided to do something creative. I sang a song about a monk who traveled around lancing people's plague boils; then I handed out knives and told the kids to act it out. A little boy got hurt." Polly put down her pen and closed the folder.

That night, Polly moved her mattress onto the floor for Milburga the Mad Minstrel and slept on her box springs. It was the first fatal step in the fait accompli that overtook us. By the time the droghte of March yielded to Aprille, Gloria had taken roote.

I kept telling myself that I ought to move into a place of my own and try to get some serious work done, but writer's curiosity held me back. Gloria was the sort of person I would have avoided before I met Polly, but now that I was stuck with her, I found myself getting interested in what made her tick.

It was frustrating; we learned almost nothing about her. Like Mélisande, she skirted inquiries about her origins with gauzy non sequiturs, and her habit of breaking into Middle English obscured whatever regional accent she might have had.

There was some talk about getting her a job, but even Polly had to admit that her appearance ruled out any possibility of a nine-to-five life, or even a midnight-to-dawn one. The most ghoulish thing about her was the way she squatted naked on her mattress and curled her hair. It was unlike any grooming operation I had ever seen, including documentaries on baboons. Instead of dividing the hair into sections and working on one at a time the way you're supposed to, she simply shoved the curling rod into her tangled web, captured any old clump, twisted it up into a knot, and pressed the button. When the steam rose, she looked like a troll on a heath.

The only normal thing she did was watch Polly's TV show, if that could be called normal. She never went out, preferring to spend the day sprawled on her mattress with purple labia to the breeze like Cleopatra's sails, strumming her lute or reading Froissart's *Chronicles* while I stenotyped Regencys. About once a week, when her yearning for the Middle Ages got too strong, she would pop some pills and escape into the past. These interludes produced some of our most bizarre conversations, like the time she yelled, "We need more friars!" and Polly said, "Isabel has a Dutch oven."

Matters remained in limbo until a fateful morning in June when the phone rang during breakfast. Polly got up to answer it. I paid no attention when I heard her say, "Oh, no!" because most of her phone calls started that way, but when she returned to the table pale and shaken, I knew something had happened.

"That was a lawyer in California. My Uncle Ezra was harpooned during a Greenpeace mission. He left everything to me in his will. His house, his royalties, and two hundred thousand dollars."

4

*There is a tide in the affairs of women which, taken at the flood,
leads God knows where.*

—Lord Byron

Uncle Ezra's demise triggered an international incident
that nearly led to World War III. In true Bradshaw fashion,
he had managed to involve not only the Japanese whaling
ship whose captain cut him in half, but an Italian merchant
vessel, a Dutch underwater exploration team, a Canadian
cruise boat full of senior citizens on their way to peaceful
Polynesia, and a Russian nuclear sub.

Only the whale escaped unscathed, "which," said Polly in an NBC interview, "was the way Uncle Ezra would
have wanted it." Never mind the nine hundred and
sixty-three lawsuits that buried The Hague in paper, or
all the people at Lloyd's who would have to work until
four a.m. for the next ten years. The Bradshaws were
happy.

Her network appearance drew a number of very good
job offers from television bigwigs who wanted her to do
a toned-down version of "Heated Topics" for them, but
she refused to have anything to do with what she called

the "co-optive Establishment." Fired by Uncle Ezra's example of selfless idealism, she shifted into high Bradshaw and decided to use her inheritance to start a feminist commune in California.

"The house he left me is in Ventura, near Los Angeles. I've never been there but I've seen pictures of it. It's huge! I want to fill it with women! It's what I've always wanted to do and now I can. I'm bursting with ideas for exciting projects! We can do so much good! We—" She broke off and looked at me uncertainly. "You'll come, won't you?"

"I wouldn't miss it for the world."

I meant just that and no more. The last thing I wanted to do was join a feminist commune, but I thought there might be a book in it that all the Women's Libbers would buy. I was willing to write it as long as I didn't have to read it.

"Me, neither," said Gloria.

In the excitement of the past week we had almost forgotten she was still with us, but now she was ours for keeps. Any hope of getting rid of her had vanished when Polly decided to embrace the entire female sex.

We decided to drive to California, so Polly turned in her car for a new Ford van. I blanched when I saw it. Having learned to drive on a low-slung sports car, I was now dead set against anything else. Like Queen Caroline, I preferred the drawers I knew to the drawers I didn't.

"It's up too high," I complained. "It doesn't have any fenders to measure by. I can't drive it."

"Yes, you can. Perkin Pritchard proved by practice," said the nattering nabob of positivism. She went on to point out the many advantages of vans.

"It can serve double duty. After we get to California and start the commune, we can use it for a mobile crisis unit. Everybody uses vans for that nowadays. Meanwhile, it'll save us money. We can take all our stuff with us instead of shipping it and paying frieght rates." Her thin lips pursed. "You know how dear they are."

A great change had come over her since she had become an heiress. She had always been thrifty, but now she was as tight as a drum. Something about having a lot of money brought out her Cap'n Nehemiah tendencies with a vengeance.

To make sure we would not have to ship anything and to prove that women were as well-organized as men, she took charge of the move down to the last detail. I was certain she was going to crack up; all of her compulsions surfaced and she started to look like Charlton Heston with jaws locked and all sphincters clenched.

First came INVENTORY OF APARTMENT CONTENTS.

"We must make lists," she instructed, a muscle in her cheek jumping. "Each of us will make a preliminary *Must Go* list and check it against a preliminary *Expendable* list. That way, we'll be able to compile a final master list of every single item in the van and devise a coded notation to tell us exactly where to find it."

Gloria's list was a model of simplicity. She had added nothing to her net worth since her arrival except a new bottle of gentian violet for her crab condition.

My list was much longer and began with something that was bound to upset Polly: Quadrupet.

"I knew it," she sighed.

"We're bonding."

Since we were taking him, we had to take his belongings, so I listed them: a scratching post the size of a small tree, a bamboo pagoda that he refused to sleep in but loved to hump, and his mobile, all gifts from me. I had made the mobile from a broom handle, a weighted Christmas tree stand, and an umbrella-style plastic clothes dryer. From the clothespins dangled strings of varying lengths tied to crumpled cigarette wrappers, which he batted at for hours on end. This unique contraption stood 4′6¾″ high—Polly measured it with her carpenter's rule—and would not fold or bend in any direction. We would have to transport it upright.

When Polly added my list to hers she nearly turned the van in on a truck. It wasn't the usual girlish problem of too many clothes. We were both unstylish in totally different ways but neither of us had a big wardrobe. We did have: six hundred books, Aunt Tabitha's suffragette banners, the Pat Nixon dartboard, the walking machine, the file cabinet, ten reams of writing paper, stenotype machine, three cartons of stenotype tape, tripod, typewriter, picket signs for all occasions, a model of the *Titanic,* and the birth bucket.

As if all of this were not enough, Polly insisted on taking the pieces of the wall.

"Leave them here," I pleaded. "Why drag along something that didn't cost anything in the first place?"

"Use it up, wear it out, make it do, or do without."

When the inventory was finished, the packing began. My method was to have a few drinks first, while I thought about packing. Then, when the thought was no longer painful, I packed. I was feeling no pain at all when I scooped up two teacups, an electric knife, my file on famous English murders, my Latin dictionary, and a bathrobe and tossed them into cardboard box.

Polly watched with mounting anguish as I stumbled around the room in my state of terminal miscellany.

"Stop it!" she shrieked. "I can't stand it! Never mind, never mind, let me do it."

That's how I got out of packing.

After she got the boxes sealed up she went to the dime store and bought so many tags and labels that I thought we would have to pack *them.* There were red tags for breakables, blue tags for soft goods, and yellow tags shaped like light bulbs with a picture of Mr. Kilowatt for electrical appliances. She bought white labels with OPEN THIS END! written in green, which were not to be confused with the blue labels that had OPEN OTHER END! written in red, nor used when the situation called for buff labels with check blocks to tell us whether the items in the box were for ☐ *Bedroom* ☐ *Dining Room* ☐ *Rec Room* ☐ *Attic.*

"Logic," she said through gritted teeth as she checked away, "is not a male quality but a human quality."

When the packing was finished she measured all the cartons and then crawled around in the back of the van armed with clipboard, slide rule, and her ever-present folding yardstick. The result was PRELIMINARY LOADING SPECIFICATIONS.

"Look," she said worriedly, pointing to some figures on her clipboard. They were $8\frac{9}{16}$ and $14\frac{5}{7}$. "What are we going to do about that?"

I shrugged. "I never add fractions if they have different bottoms."

She glared at me. "Do you know what this means? We'll have to rent a U-Haul cartop carrier."

That broke her heart but it was still cheaper than the "dear" freight rates. She drove the van down to the U-Haul depot and returned with the carrier affixed. She informed me that it held twenty cubic feet, whatever that was, and then went to work on REVISED PRELIMINARY LOADING SPECIFICATIONS.

By now the apartment was strewn with lists, all decorated with smeary black puncture marks. There was only one thing that had not happened, but I knew it would, and I was right. Around midnight, she made a list of the lists.

The day before our scheduled departure, we loaded the van according to her figures and parked it in the back alley. To make sure nobody stole it during the night, I nominated Gloria to spend the night in it and made her promise to remain vertical so that any potential thieves would be sure to see her. She said, "By my troth," spat three times through her forefinger and pinkie, and left with her lute. I watched from the window to make sure she got settled and then Polly and I went to bed.

A few minutes later, or so it seemed, the alarm went off and it was time to get up. I lurched like a beached seal and tried not to throw up; this was what Polly meant by "getting an early start." The room was pitch black. For a moment I thought I had gone blind from shock, but then Polly switched on her light, swept back her blanket with a d'Artagnan flourish, and rose.

Or tried to. Quadrupet was slung across her neck like a hairy albatross, determined to thwart what he knew was to be a violent uprooting.

"Move, slug!" she yelled.

She tried to push him away but he rolled over on her face and tried to smother her. I waited hopefully, listening to the struggle.

"ZZZZZZZZZTTTTTTTTT!"

"YEEEOOOOWWWWW!"

I peeped over the blanket and saw her sucking her arm. Quadrupet burrowed and went back to sleep.

"Get up," she said to me. "I'm bleeding to death. Where did we put the Mercurochrome?"

"In the box marked *Contents of Medicine Chests,* subdivision *Breakable.*"

It was already packed in the van. She said nothing.

According to her departure plan, we were supposed to leap out of bed, strip off the sheets, roll them up, and put them in the still-open box marked *Bed Linens.* This scenario fell apart when she accidentally rolled Quadrupet up in her mattress pad. He lurched manfully and came rolling back out again, then stalked into the kitchen and deliberately knocked over his water bowl.

I staggered into my bathroom and found it plastered with notes from Polly. DO NOT LEAVE TOILET PAPER BEHIND! was stuck on the wall facing the john at such a perfect eye level that I was sure she had measured it. When I

stood up and went to the basin to brush my teeth, there
was another note on the mirror that said REMEMBER YOUR
TOOTHBRUSH! with an arrow pointing down to my drinking
glass in case I forgot where I kept it. The third note was
under the light switch: HAVE YOU FORGOTTEN ANYTHING?

I glanced around and saw a lipstick with about one-
eighth of an inch left in the tube. In a burst of predawn
madness, I tore off the cap and scrawled STOP ME BEFORE I
KILL BRADSHAWS! across the mirror and emitted a high,
reedy cackle. "I found a use for it! Hee-hee-hee!"

"What?" she called.

"Nothing."

I went into her kitchen for breakfast and found the table laid with those prototypical examples of New England thrift known as "toots." A toot, she had told me,
was a paper twist containing the tag ends of household
staples that ordinarily get thrown away. The Yankee
goodwife prevented such Babylonian profligacy by dust-
ing the seams of flour and sugar sacks into little squares
of waxed paper, which were then secured at both ends.

Thanks to Polly's mathematical calculation of our
shopping needs for our last month chez Gioppi, all of our
staples had come to an end just in time for our departure.
Thus on this last morning there was just enough salt,
pepper, sugar, instant coffee, and powdered cream left to
make toots.

I sank down in my chair. We could not have a hot
breakfast because she had packed all the pots, pans, skil-
lets, and spatulas in the box marked *Kitchen Utensils: Met-
al.* Instead we were having hard-boiled eggs which she
had cooked the night before. She rolled one in my direction and we ate.

Mine was as dry as dust and stuck to the roof of my
mouth like a Communion wafer. I thought some pepper
might help give it some taste, but as I struggled with my
toot it exploded in my face and I had a sneezing fit. Just
then Polly unwrapped still another toot containing

Quadrupet's odorous Gourmet Kitty tuna. The smell wafted under my nose as I was trying to swallow the egg. It went down the wrong way and my air stopped.

"Do you want some peanut butter?" Polly asked. "It's nonpreservative."

I shook my head violently but she was already opening the toot. She smeared some on my half-eaten egg. The sight of the brown lump nearly finished me off.

"Make sure you eat it. It's a quick-energy food."

She was completely oblivious to my maroon face and my inability to breathe. My windpipe was so full of egg that I couldn't even inhale well enough to cough, and she was trying to plug up the rest of it with peanut butter. When at last I managed an equine wheeze she shook her head and said, "Cigarettes."

After breakfast, she dried the pan in which she had boiled the coffee water, put it in the box marked *Equipment for Refreshments While Traveling,* and picked up the thermos she had prepared for Gloria. I picked up Quadrupet and we were off.

"Good morrow, pilgrims!" Gloria greeted us.

She was wide awake all right. Her pupils were so dilated that her eyes looked black. Alarm coursed through me. She had taken uppers this time and she was in fyne fettyl forsooth.

She jumped down from the front seat and hopped around to the double doors in back with her duffelbag slung over her shoulder like one of those tinkers in fairy tales, the kind there are always three of. She climbed in the back and propped her green rubber feet on a box marked *Writing Materials: I. Fairfax.* I got in front and put Quadrupet's carrying case under my knees.

Polly started the van and pulled out of the alley. I tensed myself for one of her original observations and was not disappointed.

"California, here we come!"

As we drove west on the Massachusetts Turnpike, Gloria in transit took up her lute and treated us to a frenetic rendition of "The Varlets Set Fyre to the Bowels de Plantagenet."

When she hit the grisly part, Polly tilted up on one hip and groaned. "Gloria, do you have to sing about . . . that?"

She replied with a plinky discord and fell silent. If she couldn't sing about barbecued bungholes she would rather not sing at all.

Even when quiet she attracted a lot of attention. As we waited in line at the tollbooth, family types in Winnebagos stared at her through the window, and the toll-taker muttered "Jesus, Mary, and Joseph" when she stuck out her head and gave him a souped-up smile. It was even worse when we stopped for lunch at Denny's. The hostess took one look at her and led us to a table in the far corner. As we followed, several children pointed and one little girl burst into terrified sobs.

Naturally Gloria was not hungry but she was spitless. She ordered a pitcher of ice water and swilled it down, her eyes dancing about the room like a pair of epileptic fleas.

"Look!" she cried happily. "There's the jakes!" That was medieval for toilet.

"Do you have to go?" asked Polly.

"No! But I balled a Kotex salesman once!"

I suppose there was some tenuous connection between the two remarks but it really didn't matter; we were beyond non sequiturs by then. It was the first time Gloria had ever mentioned her sex life. I was surprised. Not that I thought she hadn't had one; the surprising part was that she remembered it.

"Did you?" I said.

"Yes! And he gave me a key! I've still got it!"

She rose, cackling like the poker-plying varlets of her *chansons,* and gave us a spastic wink. "Wish me luck!"

As she scurried off, Polly and I exchanged puzzled glances.

"Is she going to use a catheter?" she asked.

A few moments later she came bouncing back wearing a triumphant grin. "Listen!" she hissed, jingling her pockets. "Dimes! I've never seen one so full!"

"One what?"

"The Kotex machine! The salesman I balled told me the same key fits every machine in the country! It's the one they issue to ladies'-room matrons! They don't want the matrons to know it because they're afraid they'd get copies made! But the salesman let me in on the secret and gave me one! Whenever I'm short of bread, all I have to do is find a Kotex machine!"

There was nothing to do but eat lunch. Gloria had another pitcher of ice water.

A few hours later we stopped for dinner in Troy, New York. Gloria had come down enough to eat half of a grilled cheese sandwich and her pupils had shrunk back to reasonably normal size so I assumed she was too wrung out to cause any more trouble.

I was wrong. While Polly and I were paying the check she drifted into a souvenir shop attached to the restaurant. When she didn't come out, we left the restaurant and waited for her in the van. Finally we saw her trotting across the parking lot with her pockets bulging.

"Look," she said happily, starting to unload. Her take consisted of a garish ashtray inscribed "Souvenir of Troy," a paperweight with a snowfall scene, a letter-opener, a penknife, a slab of wood with scorch marks spelling out "Home Sweet Home," and—something that must have reminded her of the good old days—a plaster statue of a weeping little boy with his bare bottom in the air.

She dumped the whole business in Polly's lap. "I want you to have it," she said plangently.

I wondered if Polly would pack it all in a box marked

Shoplifted Items, but instead she shoved it haphazardly into the glove compartment and made tracks for the highway.

The problem of where to stop for the night was complicated by Gloria's appearance and Polly's thrift. Any hostelry that had corridors was automatically out because Gloria might wander down them and Polly refused to pay for corridors. Any motel that fell within the category known as "family-style" was also out because Gloria repelled families and Polly refused to pay for toilet seats wrapped in sterilized paper strips.

There was also an ideological problem. Polly had it in for several motel chains because of labor disputes of one kind or another, or because they did convention business with organizations that barred women members. I drove for over an hour in a state of exhaustion while she consulted her many lists and newsletters and said "No, not that one" each time we passed a vacancy sign.

At last we found a place that came up to her standards and down to Gloria's. It was called "Fran's Tourist Cabins."

Polly was too thrilled by the cheap price of a triple to consider the luxury of sleeping apart from Gloria so we all piled in together. The room was the pits: plastic curtains, rubbery doilies, blond thirties furniture, wall-to-wall linoleum, and a clawfoot tub.

It was my turn for a fix. I took a bottle of bourbon out of my suitcase. "Let's have some hooch. Is there anything to drink out of in this dump?"

"Look," said Gloria, pointing into the bathroom. "I see some hanaps."

I thought it meant "cockroach" but she explained that it was Middle English for cup. These were Dixie hanaps. I fetched three and poured us a round.

"Down the dovecote," Gloria toasted.

We were so tired that we killed the bottle before we

knew it. Polly belched gently and passed out. I stretched out beside her on the double bed and Gloria clambered onto the cot. Everything went black until an indeterminate time later when Polly and I awoke to sounds of violent hammering.

We lurched up and grappled drunkenly with each other before one of us managed to find the switch on the sleazy fringed lamp. Its muddy yellow glow revealed the same horrible room, but lacking now in one aspect of horror it had contained earlier: Gloria.

Her cot was empty. The hammering began again. Polly ran to the door and flung it open. "Look!" she cried, pointing into the driveway. "She's trying to get in the van!"

We ran outside and found Gloria stark naked, yanking at the double doors and yelling "Raise the portcullis in the name of the King!"

"Gloria, please come inside!"

"I hear the Plantagenet herald! Make haste to Gloucester!"

Lights were switching on in the other cabins. The manageress emerged from her office-home with her hair in curlers, followed by a burly tattooed man pulling on his pants. A few doors down, a couple who were obviously naked under their raincoats crept from their cabin and surveyed the scene with sleepy grins.

Gloria broke away from us and took off across the driveway, bellowing at the top of her lungs for Roger de Mortimer, Cob O' Northumberland, John of Gaunt, Longshanks, and the Bishop of Ely.

The three of us raced around the driveway. I was afraid she would get violent if we tried to force her back into the cabin, so I decided to use psychology on her.

"Come, fair maid of Kent!" I cried cheerily. "The Black Prince awaits thee in the royal chamber. He is come back from Crécy with a fine French lute!"

"This isn't funny, Isabel!" Polly yelled.

Several of the guests thought differently; a couple were choking. The manageress burst into a hoarse whiskey laugh and caught Gloria by the arm as she rounded the office.

"Okay, kid, okay," she chortled good-naturedly. "You just had one too many, that's all. Happens to the best of us."

"We can't raise the portcullis!"

"Chrissake, kid, you can't get nobody to fix things nowadays. The plumbers charge ten bucks an hour and don't do a goddamn thing."

Her warm, husky maternal voice did the trick. Gloria became docile and allowed herself to be led back to the cabin.

"You gals lay off the sauce now," Fran advised. "If you're hung over tomorrow, just stay in bed, don't worry about checkout time. My maid got shot last night so there won't be nobody around anyhow."

Gloria put her arms around Fran and laid her head on the woman's shoulder. "My liege lord has the pox!"

"That's nothin', you oughta see Harry's piles. Big as baseballs. Now go back to bed and sleep it off. Night-night."

Gloria fell into an exhausted sleep right away. While Polly was giving her teeth their usual one hundred strokes, I had a Coke with ammonia spirits and questioned the wisdom of gathering experience.

The next day the weather turned very hot, giving Polly a perfect excuse for suggesting an even cheaper place to spend the night.

"Let's stay at a campsite and sleep in the van!"

We pulled into a rustic area full of Winnebagos all in a circle like pioneer wagons expecting an Indian attack. After we got settled in our space, we roasted hot dogs for dinner. The sight of Gloria had a predictable effect on the God-and-country set, but other than walking past the horseshoe game in her draperies she did nothing to attract attention. She was back on downers.

When it was time for bed, she collapsed across the front seats and Polly and I went to the community bathhouse for showers. Afterward, we made our way back to the van through the unspoiled wilderness as Polly inhaled deeply and made ecologist noises about how wonderful it was to be close to the soil and back to nature. Like all agoraphobiacs, I could not have disagreed more.

To make room to sleep, we unloaded several of the cartons and Quadrupet's mobile and put them outside on the grass, then spread quilts and blankets on the floor of the van and climbed in. The campground was full of dogs, so I attached Quadrupet's leash and wound it securely around my wrist like Jewish mothers everywhere. He snuggled under my chin and we lay there in the crickety blackness with the back doors open to the warm summer air.

"Isn't this wonderful?" said Polly.

"No."

I had to pee. I had done it once in the shower but now I had to go again. I tried to think of sand and deserts but it didn't help. What to do? I had no intention of making another trip through the sylvan glade to the bathhouse. I decided to wait until Ms. Clean fell asleep and pee beside the van.

When she started snoring, I crept out with Quadrupet and felt my way in the dark until I made it around to the side facing the woods. Holding firmly to the leash with one hand, I used the other to unsnap my pajama bottoms and pull them down to my ankles. It's hard enough for a woman to pee in a squat in the dark without a cat taking up one hand, but I didn't dare let go of him. Bracing myself against the van, I managed to get into position and let fly.

Just then a rustling sound came from the woods and

the ever-alert Quadrupet sprang. The sudden movement unraveled the leash from my wrist and threw me off balance. I tumbled over in a puddle of pee and let go of him. With a howl of battle, he soared through the air like a comet and disappeared into the trees.

I panicked.

"HELP! STOP HIM!"

Polly burst out of the van, took one look at my pajama bottoms, and yelled at the top of her lungs.

"RAPE!"

"HE'S GONE INTO THE WOODS!"

"RAPE!"

It was our best acrostic conversation yet. Each time I yelled something like "We've got to catch him," she thought I meant a man and yelled "Rape."

Lights were switching on in the surrounding campers. Quickly, I pulled up my pajama bottoms.

"I'm all wet!" I wailed.

"Don't destroy the evidence! You must not wash yourself. Promise me you won't wash yourself. You're experiencing a felt need to counteract perceived self-disgust, but therapy will take care of that. RAPE!"

"Will you shut up?"

"Hand me my shotgun, Mabel," said a voice from the next campsite.

Soon we were surrounded by Middle Americans, all armed to the teeth and all ears as Polly babbled about blood tests, semen stains, and the morning-after pill. She was so completely beside herself that it was several minutes before I finally got through to her.

"I haven't been raped! It's Quadrupet. He's escaped!"

I threw myself against the man with the shotgun so he would not fire into the woods.

"Don't shoot! You'll hit the Quad!"

While he was figuring that out, a terrible smell filled the air. The underbrush crackled and suddenly Quadrupet was back, hissing, spitting, and snarling with rage.

"Aw, he's been sprayed by a skunk," said the man with the gun. "There's an old hunter's remedy for it, little lady."

Polly gave him a murderous glance when she heard the diminutive but I was all ears as I held the stinking Quadrupet.

"Tomato juice'll do the trick. Takes away the sting and the smell."

Fortunately, we had some in the box marked *Quick Energy Snacks.* Polly opened a can and I put Quadrupet on the ground, where he lurched in place and howled on a high, shrill zitherlike note, the kind of sound the movies use to indicate the entrance of a lunatic. She handed me the can and I tipped it over him, then stopped. I was afraid the shock of coming in contact with liquid would kill him.

"I can't do it," I whispered.

"You've got it," said the hunter. "It's the only way."

It was straight out of James M. Cain. I took a deep breath and poured. Quadrupet exploded in renewed fury and leaped two feet off the ground.

"Wrap him in lots of towels," said the hunter. "Keep 'em tight around him so's he can't lick hisself."

We ripped open *Towels* and I swathed him in three of them and cradled him in my arms. Now he looked like the sheik he wished he were.

"His little heart," I wept. "I can feel it pounding through all these towels." Now that he was safe I lost all control and began sobbing and singing at the same time. "Q-Q-Q-Quad-Quad, sweet little Quad-Quad, him's the only c-c-c-cat that I adore. When the m-m-moon shines over the mousehole, I'll be waiting at the k-k-k-kitchen door. . . ."

It was "our" song. As I strode up and down in my wet pajamas singing to the struggling bundle clutched to my bosom, the hunter looked from Quadrupet's mobile to Polly's *Free Women Now!* bumper sticker and shook his head.

When I caught her eye, there was a most unsisterly look on her face. I could practically see the urge-to-kill dagger of the comic strips hovering over her head. The stoned Gloria slept through it all.

I was at the wheel when we crossed the California line. Polly gave a cheer and suggested we celebrate by stopping for tacos.

I pulled into a low-slung ultramodern drive-in full of teenagers, station wagons full of children, and carhops in hotpants. The day was a scorcher so I looked for a shady parking space under the roof. Spying one, I made a beeline for it but we never got there. Suddenly, there was a horrible crash that left the van quivering from the impact.

"What did you do?" Polly yelled.

"I don't know!" There was nothing in front of us; no rail, no wall, no other cars, nothing. But I had hit something.

Polly and I got out and inspected the front end, then peered underneath to see if the drive shaft had broken, but all was well.

"Maybe you hit a garbage can and it rolled away," Polly suggested.

I glanced around the lot but there was nothing resembling a garbage can or any other demolished metallic object. I began to feel spooked. Had I hit an electronic eye? Maybe we had won one of those prototypical California contests involving the one-millionth taco.

Just then we noticed that everybody was staring at us. That in itself was not unusual by this time, but these stares were different from the furtive kind we were used to after traveling with Gloria. They were open and unabashed and full of a kind of simple-minded admiration. Two carhops had stopped dead in their tracks with trays poised and mouths open; the customers had all stopped eating and some of the kitchen staff had come out of the back door to watch us. Everyone seemed awestruck.

They were all looking up.

"Oh, no! The U-Haul!"

I had forgotten it was on top of the van. Now it almost wasn't. It hung by two screws, its legs twisted like melted hairpins. I had plowed right into the low-slung, ultramodern California roof.

Just then it emitted a grinding belch and started to slide.

"Catch it!" Polly screamed.

We reached up just in time. As we stood there bracing and heaving, Gloria grabbed her lute, jumped out of the van, and started running round in circles shouting useless directions. A wave of hysteria passed over me. I thought of those photos tourists have taken of themselves pretending to hold up the Leaning Tower of Pisa. I thought of Sisyphus and his rock and the little Dutch boy with his finger in the dyke. A vision formed and I saw us standing there forever like a pair of caryatids, condemned to spend eternity holding up the U-Haul while Gloria danced around us like the strophe of a Dionysian chorus.

"Stop laughing!" Polly yelled.

I was so overcome I dropped my end. The door flew open and, like a piñata, the U-Haul spewed forth gifts. *Published Works: I. Fairfax, Footwear: P. Bradshaw, Glasswear & Misc. Breakables, Rape-Prevention Brochures,* a ☐ for the attic, another ☐ for the dining room, and a ten-pound sack of Kitty Litter that burst like a bomb.

As Polly and I ducked and ran for cover, all of the people who had been watching us broke into applause. A carhop rushed up to us holding out her order pad.

"Can I have your autographs?"

"Autographs?" we said dumbly.

"Aren't you celebrities?"

A teenage boy stood up in a convertible. "Hey, where's the camera? I wanna wave to my girl."

"Are they hiring?" asked the carhop. "My agent is William Morris."

A fat woman in short-shorts leaped out of her station wagon and galloped toward us, bellowing like a sow in rut.

"I got here first! I win! Where's the giveaway?"

"It was real!" I said. "Real!"

The carhop frowned quizzically. "You mean it was a publicity stunt?"

They refused to believe that we hadn't done it on purpose. The carhop kept following us around with her pencil, pleading for an autograph, so to shut her up and get rid of her I scrawled *I. Fairfax* on her order pad.

"I knew you were a famous person," she said happily.

"Listen, I want my giveaway! I'm entitled!"

"Oh, shit," said the teenager. "Nobody got killed."

"What about the weirdo that the U-Haul fell on?" asked the giveaway lady. "She must be dead."

"No, she's the stunt girl," said the carhop knowledgeably. "She knows how to let things fall on her."

That made us remember Gloria. We turned around to the wreckage and saw a pile of boxes with an arm sticking out. At the end of it was a hand holding the lute up to safety like a battleflag.

We hurried over and pulled the stuff off of her. It was hard to tell whether she was hurt or not: she looked the same as always.

"Are you okay?"

"Urban despair!"

"Is that the name of the show?" asked the carhop.

"Gimme that guitar! That must be my freebie!"

By the time we got rid of our entourage, called the U-Haul office, and repacked the van we were too exhausted to drive on to Uncle Ezra's house. We decided to stay overnight where we were and finish our pilgrimage in the morning.

"There's a motel right across the street," I said. "They've got a vacancy sign. Come on."

But it was not to be that simple. Prudence Patience puckered. "They look much too dear. See their sign? Color TV, swimming pool, sauna, banquet rooms. No, that's sinful waste."

Near tears from strain, I offered to pay for everybody but it did no good. By now she was tight with my money, too. Nothing would do except the YWCA so off we went.

When we finally found it, she even haggled there until they agreed to create a triple room with a wheeled cart that looked as if it had seen service at the morgue. I had to sneak Quadrupet in concealed in my suitcase. I was afraid he would smother before we got upstairs so I had to punch holes in it. This was Polly's idea of saving money.

The Y was too poor to paint but not too proud to whitewash. I had to put on my sunglasses before I could flop down on one of their hard narrow beds and stare at the ceiling.

As I lay there thinking about dark cocktail lounges there was a knocking at the door. It was so soft we barely heard it, but when it came again I recognized something that my father had taught me.

The Morse code for S.O.S.

5

*Why should I remain in a country that is on the verge of
Prohibition and Women's Suffrage?*
                                        —Ambrose Bierce

The knock came again. I threw a blanket over Quadrupet. "Gloria, you answer it," I said. *That'll fix 'em.*

She opened the door a crack. "Lancaster or York?" she
demanded.

"I've got to see Polly Bradshaw right away!" hissed a
voice on the other side. "I'm in trouble!"

Gloria and I exchanged a look of shock. In our separate
ways we both preferred legends that linger to reputa-
tions that precede.

Polly stepped forward and clanged like the firebell in
the night. "I'm Polly Bradshaw. How can I help?"

Gloria opened the door all the way. The woman on the
threshold looked like a Lufthansa travel poster come to
life: the original flaxen-haired zaftig Mädchen, except
that she was in her late thirties. As tall as Polly and
about seventy pounds heavier, she was what grandmoth-
ers called "the picture of health" until you got to her
eyes. Then she changed from zaftig Mädchen to giant
panda. I had never seen such a pair of shiners. She

looked as if she had gone fifteen rounds with the Great John L.

She scurried into the room and gazed at Polly as if she were a shrine.

"I saw you on the news when your uncle was harpooned and you said you were going to start a women's commune. I recognized you downstairs in the lobby when you checked in. Are you going to start the commune soon? Because I have no place to go and no money. I ran away from my husband yesterday and I've never had a job in my life because I was married at eighteen and I don't know what to do!"

She broke off and sobbed. Gloria reached into her money belt and took out her traveling drugstore.

"Up or down?"

"Never mind that," Polly said, giving her some coins. "Here. Run down the hall to the soft drink machine and get us some Cokes. Don't put anything in them, just Cokes."

Gloria trotted off and returned a few minutes later with four Cokes and a bulging money belt. She refunded Polly's change and handed the cans around with a grand gesture.

"This is on me. They've got lots of Kotex machines here," she said happily.

Polly turned to her new project. "Now," she began in her officious tone, "what's your name?"

"Agnes Mulligan, but I want to change it so that Boomer—that's my husband—won't be able to find me." Her swollen lids stretched open in painful awe. "He can find anything; he's a survivalist."

That did it. Polly's lips pursed for battle as she contemplated the worst enemy a Bradshaw ever had: the social Darwinist. If the Boomer Mulligans of America ever got their way, there would be nobody left for her to help.

"He beat me with his divining rod," Agnes went on. "And when I told him I didn't want to spend our vacation in the bomb shelter he built, he shot arrows at me."

"A crossbow?" Gloria asked.

"No, the regular kind. But he's got a crossbow for mountain lions."

"Does it have—"

"Never mind the crossbow," Polly said impatiently. "Did you file an assault charge against him?"

"Oh, mercy, no! He would have killed me for sure."

"Do you have any children?"

"Not with me. Two boys at home. They're survivalists, too. They had their hearts set on vacationing in the bomb shelter. When I said I didn't want to, they zipped me up in a sleeping bag and left me like that for ten hours. I wet myself," she added abashedly.

"How did you get free?"

"The attack dogs accidentally rescued me. They got hysterical—they always get hysterical after a training lesson—and started ripping up everything they could find. They found my bag."

Her blue-black face screwed up for another round of tears. "We had an Irish wolfhound before, but he was too friendly so Boomer shot him."

"How could he hurt an animal?" I said indignantly. Polly gave me a dirty look.

"I would have left him a long time ago," Agnes went on, "but I didn't know how to do it without money. He never let me have a cent."

"He refused to give you a housekeeping allowance?" Polly asked.

"No, it wasn't that. He just went off money. All the survivalists in his group did. They put their wives on the barter system and made us trade with each other. Boomer said it was a good way to practice for *der Tag*— that's his name for when the lights go out and everybody takes to the hills."

"How did you manage to run away?"

"I stole his Raleigh coupons."

The two nonsmokers looked blank so Agnes explained. "They're premium coupons you get with Raleigh cigarettes. Like green stamps. Boomer and all the other survivalists switched to Raleighs so they could save the coupons and redeem them for a year's supply of freeze-dried disaster food for the bunker they're building. Boomer was in charge of the coupons. He kept them in our spare room. So yesterday when he and the boys were out shopping for an elephant gun, I packed up all the coupons and left. I drove all the way from Denver without stopping except to buy gas. I still have a Shell card he forgot to take away from me, and there was some money in the glove compartment that he kept for tolls."

"I don't understand what good the coupons are to you," Polly said. "Are you planning to sell the stuff you get for them?"

"Oh, no. You can redeem them for cash, too. They're worth three-quarters of a cent apiece."

"How many do you have?"

"Six suitcases."

She took us down the hall to her room and showed us her loot. There were Raleigh coupons everywhere. The six huge pieces of manly brown luggage she had also stolen from Boomer were overflowing with them, and so were her various tote bags and make-up kits.

"I haven't had a chance to count them yet," Agnes said.

"We'll help you," Polly volunteered for us. "It won't take long if we all count together. We've got plenty of cardboard boxes; we'll give you some to pack them in and have them ready for mailing tomorrow!"

"Do you have to lick them and put them in a book?" Gloria asked warily.

"No, just count them."

"All right, let's get to work," Polly said briskly.

"Let's eat first," I countered. "Agnes must be hungry, and we never did get around to tacos, remember?"

She agreed reluctantly. Agnes and I locked up our respective treasures—Raleigh coupons and Quadrupet— and the four of us went downstairs.

Naturally, Polly wanted to eat in the Y cafeteria. "Why go out when there's a perfectly good—"

"Because I need a drink!" I snapped.

"Wait a minute," said Gloria as we moved toward the exit, "there's a jakes in the lobby." She squished off on her green rubber feet and was back a few minutes later with another bulge in her moneybelt.

"Dinner's on me," she said grandly.

We found a steak house with a Happy Hour sign. As we walked in I girded myself for the usual stares but nobody gave us a second glance. We were in southern California now, home of the giant panda and the Army surplus troll.

"Hi," said the hostess. "You from the Little Theater?" She herself was tattooed. She seated us at big table in the middle of the room and handed around menus.

Gloria cased the joint quickly and rose. "I'm going to the jakes."

As she squished off, Agnes wrinkled her nose. "I wish she'd call it the little girls' room, don't you?" she whispered.

"The *women's* room," Polly corrected.

Gloria returned triumphant and we ordered drinks. Since somebody else was buying, Polly ordered a Chivas Regal sour. Agnes chose one of those eggwhite-and-liqueur messes favored by nondrinkers, and I had a double bourbon on the rocks. Gloria had a pitcher of ice water.

Agnes took a sip of her drink and then stared down into its frothy pink depths. It was the "seeking answers" pose of the movie drunk but it didn't work with a Strawberry Cadillac Flip. Not even Ray Milland could have pulled it off.

"I've got to have a new identity before I redeem the Raleigh coupons," she said. "I don't dare send them in under my real name because Boomer knows I have them. I'm afraid he'd contact the Raleigh people and trace me through them." She chewed on her thumbnail and cast a furtive glance over her shoulder. "Do you think it would attract less attention if I packed them in lots of little boxes and mailed them gradually?"

"Agnes," Polly said supportively, "forget the Raleigh coupons for a minute and concentrate on one thing at a time. Now, let's look at your problem logically. One: you have disappeared. Two: you must *stay* disappeared. Three: to effect the above, you need a new name. Therefore, we must deal with three first."

While she was being logical, I analyzed the situation along subjective lines. However many aliases Agnes used, her chances of disappearing successfully into anything except the chorus of *Die Walküre* were virtually nil. If she stayed underground long she would become graffiti's newest sensation. *Judge Crater, please call your office, your secretary has found Agnes. . . . Vacationing writer Ambrose Bierce locates runaway housewife. . . . Little Charley Ross laid Big Agnes Mulligan.*

I decided her best bet was to become a female impersonator. The safest hiding place, said Poe, is the most obvious one. The gay boys would be mad for her.

Polly rapped the table authoritatively. "All right, what's Agnes's new name going to be? Everybody will make a suggestion and then we'll vote. Isabel?"

"Ex Parte Mulligan."

Agnes gave me a pensive frown that was hauntingly familiar. "That's nice," she said politely, "but I want to change my last name, too."

"Gloria? What do you think?" Polly asked.

"I balled a draft evader and he said that when you change your name you should stick to your ethnic group because little idiosyncrasies can give you away."

That didn't sit well with the Great Equalizer. She firmly believed that nobody would ever take either of us for a Wasp unless we told them.

"What are you, Agnes?" I asked.

"Welsh. My maiden name was Owen."

"How about Llanfairpwllgwngllgogferychywll?" Gloria suggested.

Another pensive frown. Then: "That's a little too long."

I choked and dribbled bourbon down my front. She was going to make a great feminist.

Polly glared at me. "How about Rhondda?" she said.

Geography was the only interesting subject she knew anything about, thanks to the Bradshaw penchant for international labor movements. Grandfather Lyman, I recalled now, had been thrown down a mine shaft in Wales.

"Double *d* in Welsh is pronounced *th*," Gloria advised, "but most people don't know dat."

Now we both got a glare. As they weighed the merits of Davies and Morgan, I tried to think of Welsh idiosyncrasies that might give Agnes away. She wasn't going to crack coal or sing in a male chorus, and God knows she didn't lilt.

"Agnes," I said, "why don't you become Swedish?"

"Come to think of it, people have always asked me if I was Swedish," she replied in flattered tones. "Okay, let's pick out a Swedish name."

"The draft evader said you should keep the same initials because capital letters are the most automatic and individual marks of penmanship," Gloria said.

I snapped my fingers. "Astrid Mortensen!"

"I like that," said Polly. "All in favor say aye."

It was unanimous. "Good! It's anonymous." She turned to Agnes. "Well, Astrid, how do you feel?"

Silence fell like a pall as Agnes stared down into her frothy depths. "What?" she said with a start. "Oh. I'm fine, thanks." Her bruised eyes looked furtively around the restaurant. "Suppose some postal worker who smokes Raleighs recognizes the address on the packages and steals them? Just taking that many Raleigh coupons to the post office will attract attention, won't it? They're bound to know it's something valuable. How could I prove they were mine if they get stolen?"

"Insure them," I said.

"Then there'll be a record!"

"Jésu. . . ." Gloria muttered.

"Agnes, listen," Polly said patiently. "You haven't done anything illegal—"

"If I send the coupons in under Astrid Mortensen, how will I cash the check when it comes? I don't have any I.D. for my new name."

"Just bring it to me; I'll take care of it. Remember, we're sisters. I wouldn't *let* you go to a bank."

While the reassurances piled up, Gloria opened her money belt and went to work piling dimes, building an elaborate replica of a medieval castle on the restaurant check. When she finished, she looked up at the astonished waitress and gave her a blurry smile.

"Vegas."

We returned to the Y and gathered in Agnes's room for the Raleigh coupon count. It soon became obvious that we were in for a long dark night of the soul. Having never done anything remotely wrong in her entire conventional life, she had, in just forty-eight hours, left her husband, stolen his Raleigh coupons, and taken an alias. Awash in guilt, she had to do something right and proper to bring order into her now-disorderly life. This meant knowing *exactly* how many Raleigh coupons she had. The goodness, the purity of being absolutely honest with the Brown and Williamson Tobacco Company had become the touchstone of her sanity.

I started things off on the wrong foot by suggesting a

shortcut. "Why don't I go down to the van and get my postage scale? We can figure out how many there are to the ounce and weigh them instead of counting them."

"Oh, no! We can't do that!" she cried. "You see," she explained, looking at me with desperate eyes, "when you tear the coupons off, sometimes a little paper from the pack sticks to them. That could make them weigh more!"

Nor would she count them fifty or a hundred at a time and then add up the grand total. Anything other than a running consecutive count was also a shortcut, and the very word conjured up unspeakable extralegal abominations.

So the four of us sat there muttering "twenty-six thousand four hundred thirty-four . . . twenty-six thousand four hundred thirty-five . . ." until well past midnight.

When Polly, Gloria, and I finished our stacks and gave her the totals, her blackened eyes swam with doubt.

"Are you sure?" she whispered hoarsely.

"Postive," we chorused.

"It's not that I don't trust you," she began, talking through her well-gnawed thumbnail. "I'm grateful for your help, but . . . you see, I have to be sure! Sure in my own mind! I can't be at peace with myself unless I know! Please try to understand. I've got to live with myself, to look at myself every morning in the mirror." She screwed up her face and sobbed. "Don't hate me! It's just that I have to *know of my own knowledge!*"

"Jésu. . . ."

So Agnes counted our coupons all over again while we stacked the absolutely-positivelies in the cartons Polly brought up from the van. She, of course, was actually enjoying the countdown, waiting eagerly for the grand total so she could figure out how much X times $3/4$¢ amounted to. She had her string and masking tape at the ready, aching for the moment when she could start tying and labeling some new boxes.

Around four in the morning, Agnes announced that she had *exactly* 61,345 Raleigh coupons. Polly reached for her Magic Marker and the tying began. Gloria and I staggered forward to contribute our thumbs and then collapsed in the Y's dismal boudoir chairs.

The cartons were no sooner tied up than Agnes started to worry.

"Did I put a slip of paper containing my name and address in each one? You're supposed to do that when you mail packages, in case it rains on the return address and they can't read it. It's in the postal regulations manual."

"I saw you do it, Agnes," I mumbled. "You put a slip of paper in each box with your name and the address of Polly's new house."

"I can't remember doing it! I've got to be *sure!* I can't be at peace unless I'm absolutely sure!"

She reopened all the boxes. Sure enough, there was a slip of paper with all the necessary information in each one. When she had satisfied herself that they were *really* there, Polly retied the boxes and Gloria and I assisted. I had heard of people going to sleep on their feet but we went to sleep on our thumbs.

At last it was finished. Absolutely finished once and for all the final time. We all crashed in Agnes's room. Three hours later, I dreamed that a firm hand was shaking my shoulder and a chowdery voice was saying "Rise and shine." I woke up and there she was, fresh and alert and wearing a new denim pants suit. I rubbed the sticky out of my eyes and looked in the mirror. I looked like Mother Goddam. Gloria, who looked dead on normal occasions, now looked exhumed.

"Hurry," Polly said. "We have to get Agnes's boxes to the post office as soon as it opens."

"Stamps cost the same all day long. Let me sleep."

"You can't. We have a busy day ahead of us. I have to stop by the lawyer's office and get the keys to the house."

We checked out and lugged the boxes downstairs. When we got out to the parking lot, the question arose of which vehicle to use. The van was too full and Agnes's Impala was too hot.

She wrung her hands and started to cry again. "That's Boomer's car! It's in his name, everything's in his name! He must have reported me missing by now. If we use his car and they catch us in it, they'll impound the Raleigh coupons!"

"I balled a car fence," said Gloria. "Switch the plates. Later on, we can paint the Impala a different color and I'll show you how to screw up the registration so you can sell it."

"Oh mercy! That's illeg—"

"Do it," Gloria cut in. I looked at her with new respect.

Polly found her tool chest and handed out shining screwdrivers. We put the Colorado plates on the van and the Massachusetts ones on the Impala and climbed in.

Polly drove. I sat in the buddy seat with Quadrupet, and Gloria and Agnes wedged themselves into the back with the boxes. Agnes looked like a French aristocrat in a tumbril. In a few moments she would have to entrust her Raleigh coupons to strangers. Could she do it? Or would she have a convulsion in the post office?

When we finally found a parking place near the post office, Agnes emitted a piteous wail and clutched her head.

"Did I put Agnes Mulligan or Astrid Mortensen on the slips of paper inside? I can't remember! Oh, wait, I've got to be sure!"

"Agnes!" Gloria yelled. "Don't touch that string! You're going to mail those fucking boxes right now or else!"

Polly's mouth dropped open. Sisters weren't supposed to curse at each other. It worked, though. Agnes became a changed woman at once. Her husband had hollered at her so much it was all she knew. Putting on her sunglasses to hide her black eyes, she hefted a carton and walked into the post office. We followed with the rest and everybody got in line. Absolutely nothing wild 'n' woolly happened. Agnes spoke to the clerk in a cordial, businesslike manner. When he handed her the insurance receipt she tucked it into her wallet and put the wallet back in her purse without checking five times to see if she had *really* put it back.

When the clerk took the cartons to the back room, she did not go around to the alley and peer in the mailroom window to see if he was stealing them. She did not try to hide on a truck, or express a desire to go out to the airport and spy on the cargo loading.

It was, I thought nostalgically, the most normal example of human behavior I had seen for a long time.

Later that afternoon, we were bumping along a winding road with the sound of the sea in our ears. I was at the wheel of Agnes's car, following Polly and Gloria in the van. As we climbed the hill to Uncle Ezra's house, I figured Gloria must be saying "This castle hath a pleasant seat," so I said "Manderley" and Agnes said "Who?" to go with what undoubtedly was Polly's "What?"

It was the biggest house I had ever seen, with all sorts of Queen Anneish things dripping and hanging and thrusting all over it. There were three full stories, plus an attic, veranda, turret, and widow's walk. The back practically hung out over the sea.

We all got out and said "Well, here we are" several times. Then a silence fell, which Gloria promptly filled.

"It looks like the house in *Psycho.*"

6

A cat has nine lives and a woman has nine cat's lives.
—Thomas Fuller

Polly walked through the house inhaling the salty air and exclaiming "Isn't this wonderful?" until she got to the cellar. When she came back upstairs, one look at her ashen face told me that Quadrupet was going to have meaningful work at last.

We unloaded the van and got our room assignments. There were plenty of rooms to choose from and several had private baths, so it was a good start on the road to liberty, equality, and sisterhood. Now I wouldn't have to watch Gloria do her creepy hair-curling act or listen to Polly's diarrhealike mantra.

After we had unpacked, we gathered round the kitchen table for a planning session.

"Now," Polly began, then stopped. From the cellar came a swift, sure thud, followed by a piteous cry of "eek!" that was broken off in mid-eek. Polly tried to hide her swallow with her turtleneck, but I saw her throat move. Agnes, ultrafeminine like most big women, gathered in imaginary skirts and looked around at the baseboards for holes. We were all terrified of rodents except Gloria, who liked life best when it included plague. She was smiling her blurry smile, undoubtedly imagining herself driving around in the van singing "Bring Out Your Dead."

"Now," Polly began again. "I want to call us the Don't Tread on Me Women's Commune. All in favor say aye."

It was unanimous. "Now," she went on, "I think we should be completely self-sufficient. I move that we grow our own vegetables and keep poultry. Let's have some discussion. The floor is open."

"Boomer made me put in a garden," said Agnes. "I can do that."

"Can I be the goose girl?" asked Gloria.

"Wonderful!" Polly effused. Things were working out along the selflessly cooperative lines that she cherished. I didn't volunteer for anything because we had already decided that I was to be the commune cook. Not that there was much choice in the matter: Polly considered it a point of honor to be a bad cook, Agnes had forgotten all she knew about cooking from living with males who wanted nothing but roots and berries, and Gloria had barely acquired the knack of eating.

"I wonder," Polly mused, caressing her chin, "if we should get a pig?"

"Aye!" Gloria cried, her eyes blazing with ecstasy. Life on a medieval barony.

"What do you want with a pig?" I asked irritably.

"To save on garbage collection. Do you know what they charge to come all the way out here?"

Agnes, who had long since learned to accept any scheme involving rugged individualism, however outlandish, went along with the pig idea, so I was outvoted.

After the strategy session, Polly and I drove to the supermarket to stock up on provisions. Naturally, we got into the running argument we always had when we shopped together: my "we must have butter" and her "margarine's good enough." She also bought sixty-watt lightbulbs to replace the hundred-watters already in the house. I knew she would have us down to twenty-five watts before too long so I bought some of my own energy-crammed brand when she wasn't looking.

By the time we finished our first dinner at the house we were all so sleepy that we voted to go to bed. As we made the Himalayan trek to our rooms, I decided that the staircase was the kind that Olivia de Havilland would mount once, and then never come down again. Giving my best dry cackle, I delivered the signature line from *The Heiress.*

"I can be very cruel. I was taught by masters."

Agnes screamed and shrank against the newel post.

"Stop saying silly things," Polly snapped.

My room was bigger than both Gioppi apartments put together. I was all set to enjoy the first privacy I had known since the wall collapsed when I heard a timid knock at the door. I opened it and found a quavering Agnes hugging her pillow and trailing blankets.

"I'm afraid to sleep by myself," she bleated. "I used to sleep with my sister before I was married, and then I slept with Boomer, so I've never been alone at night before and I'm scared. Would you let me sleep on your couch?"

I bent my head back and gazed up at her tear-stained face. Somewhere inside this 160-pound Juno was a fragile, petite girl who kept coming out. I was too tired to put up a fight so I waved her onto the couch. After spreading her blankets with great care and plumping her pillow for an interminable length of time—an unfailing sign of the insomniac—she crashed down on my couch.

"Do you mind leaving the light on?" she whimpered, as I was about to turn it off. "It's not that I'm afraid of the dark, I just don't like it." I left it on.

"Talk to me," she pleaded. "My sister and I used to talk each other to sleep."

I suppose if I hadn't been an only child I would have known how to handle the situation, but I was used to entertaining myself in introverted ways. So help me, I didn't mean to do it; I was just casting around for a topic of conversation.

"Look," I said, gazing up at the paint patterns on the ceiling. "There's a man in an Australian bush hat with a big mustache."

"OH, GOD! OH, NO! HELP! HELP MEEEEEEE!"

Polly bounded in. "What's the matter?"

Agnes raised a shaking arm and pointed to the window and the widow's walk beyond. "He's there!"

"Don't move!" Polly ordered. "Stay where you are and pretend there's nothing wrong. Don't show fear! Repeat, *don't show fear!* They always hurt passive women more— that's victimology!"

"Polly—" I began.

"Shh!" She pretended to smile nonchalantly while she talked out of the side of her mouth. "Is he on the widow's walk?"

"There isn't—"

"The best way is to wait until they're about to do it, then pee on them. It's called the disgust factor. We had a lecture on it by a psychologist at the Self-Sufficiency Center during Anti-Rape Week. Crapping is even better. Do you have to go?"

"THERE ISN'T ANY MAN ON THE WIDOW'S WALK!" I yelled. "HE'S ON THE CEILING!"

They both regarded me with expressions of atavistic fear. I felt like the Thing in a Thing movie.

"The ceiling?"

"Yes! In the paint!"

"In the paint?"

"In the marks left by the brush. You can see pictures

in them. Didn't you ever lie in bed when you were little
and make pictures out of the paint sworls?"

"No," Polly said scornfully.

"I should have known better than to ask. Look, come
here. See? He's between the Gainsborough lady and the
Indian chief."

Smirking, she humored me with a theatrical display of
twisting and bending as she gave the ceiling a mock inspection.

"I don't see a thing. It's all in your imagination."

I collapsed in the direction of the bed, missed it, and
rolled on the floor.

"What's so funny?" she asked suspiciously.

"It *is* my imagination!"

She frowned pensively. "That's what I said."

"Oh, Jesus!"

"You know, Isabel"—she sighed, shaking her head—"I
think you're going slowly crazy."

"Don't worry, I'll get there eventually."

She turned and started for the door, then stopped and
pursed her lips as she surveyed the ceiling. "But you're
right about one thing," she said generously. "That ceiling
does need repainting. I'll do it with a roller so you'll stop
seeing things."

She looked at Agnes. "Are you all right now?"

"Yes. It's just that I thought she meant Boomer. He has
one of those Australian hats. I thought he had come after
me."

We finally got to sleep, but the next morning we had
another crisis when Agnes found a pile of dead rats outside my door.

"Quadrupet put them there," I said craftily. "He loves
me best, so he brings his kill to my room."

That's how I got rid of her. Between men on the ceiling and rats in the doorway, she developed an instant
preference for sleeping alone.

After breakfast we drove into town to shop for seeds and the lumber Polly needed to build a pigsty and a chicken yard. She also arranged for a phone. I stood by the door of the pay booth and listened with grudging admiration to the wrangle. I had to hand it to her; like most people I was putty in the hands of a Ma Bell service representative.

"We have eight bedrooms, drawing room, parlor, dining room, cellar, attic, eat-in kitchen, walk-in pantry, wrap-around veranda, three-car garage, and a detached workshop. Yes, that's what I said: *one* desk phone. What? Don't worry, a little walking never hurt anybody. One, repeat *one*, desk phone. How much is the push-button? Never mind, I'll take a circular dial. One *black* desk phone with a circular dial. How much is the extra extension cord? *What?* I can do without it. I'm neither sugar nor salt, I won't melt. Chimes? Nope. A plain ring'll do."

She hung up and emerged from the booth. "They must be ready for nationalization after that," I said.

"It's coming," she said solemnly. "It has to."

Next we went to the public library, where I took out a card so Polly could check out the books she needed but refused to buy: gripping sagas like *How to Build Your Own Chicken Coop* and *Pigs for Profit*. When she had made her selection, I mentioned that *The Egg and I* contained much useful information. I found a copy and handed it to her. She read the jacket flaps and the extracted quotes on the back with a critical air, then looked at me with all systems pursed.

"All right, but I don't want to read the whole book. Can you go through it and mark the serious parts for me?"

The next few days were a nightmare of leveling and beveling as the greatest carpenter since you-know-Who fashioned henhouse, pigsty, and trough. I did a little work on my latest Regency, "Rake of Hearts," but it was impossible to concentrate while the Liberated Kid was slinging nails. I gave up and put on my windbreaker and sneakers and took a walk along the beach to think important thoughts. I looked very Kennedyish, except that I had only thirty-two teeth and the kind of pallor usually associated with convicts.

I couldn't believe that I had actually consented to be a member of a women's commune in southern California. I liked states with early seventeenth-century tombstones; if a tombstone is still readable, somebody is being avant garde. As for gathering experience, it was turning into a mad literary dig without a protective pith helmet or wise native guides to say "Memsahib rest now." Life with Polly had given me absolutely nothing to write about that the feminists would like, though Alfred Hitchcock might.

I sat down on a rock and made my decision: I would take Quadrupet and go. Just where I wasn't sure, but as I thought about it, I decided on New Orleans. It was the South, which was important to me, and even more important, they had *sixteenth*-century tombstones.

I stood up full of resolve and went to tell Polly, but when I got to the outbuildings the livestock had arrived. One look at the chickens was proof that Betty MacDonald had been right about their personality problems: they just weren't responsive.

The pig was another matter. He was black and white with pink showing through, and smaller than I had expected. He looked frightened in his new, sparkling clean surroundings. Would Polly insist on keeping the pigpen clean? Yes, she would. I reached out and gave him a comforting pat.

"Him is Mommy's perfect poo-poo, yes him is. Oh, I see him eyes crinkling! Him smiles-smiles, yes him does!"

"Isabel—"

"Him is Farnsworth! That him new name-names." He

nuzzled my muddy sneaker. Polly put her hands on her hips and rolled her eyes.

"You don't name pigs. Honestly, Isabel, sometimes I think you like animals better than *people*."

"I do. 'The more I see of Mankind, the more I prefer my dog.' "

I saw the pensive frown start to grow and knew she was getting ready to say "I don't see what dogs have to do with it," so I warded her off before she could get it out.

"It's a quotation from Blaise Pascal."

"Never heard of him. Will you stop hugging that pig?"

"Does him want him own song-songs like Quadrupet? All right, Mommy wrote song-songs for hims. Hail to thee, O noble Farnsworth, lying in the swill! Though about him flies do gather, Mommy loves him still!"

"Isabel, he is not, repeat *not*, a pet! He's our garbage disposal."

"He's a human being and he has a right to be treated like one."

She went off shaking her head and I went off to the feed-and-grain store to buy Farnsworth a sack of Red Dog to mix with his garbage so he would not be hungry. My moving plans faded in the sunshine of his beady-eyed smile.

We had another planning session, at which we decided to perfect our self-sufficiency before throwing open the doors of Don't Tread on Me to the female public at large.

I did my part by "retraining Agnes to enter the marketplace," as Polly called it. I called it teaching her stenotype. When I offered to do it, Polly looked at me with missionary pride and said "I think that's *fine*" in her stout voice. I knew she thought I was turning into a feminist so I let her think it, but my real motives were as ulterior as ever.

In short, I was in the throes of a writing block. I was so

sick of Regencys I couldn't bear the thought of writing another, so I figured that if I lent Agnes the stenotype machine I would have a perfect excuse for cutting myself off from the whole Ravenshaven madhouse. To clear my conscience further, I lent Polly my typewriter. With Agnes struggling through beginning fingering and muttering "HR-L" and Polly hammering out incoherent manifestos on rape, I was free at last.

It was my first block, so I decided to relax and enjoy it. The first thing I enjoyed was getting up in the morning without brushing close to death. As soon as I stopped writing I was able to cut down to two packs a day without even trying; I no longer suffered from spontaneous gagging and could hack comfortably in a ladylike fashion without losing my breath.

After shoveling up the night's catch of dead rats, I went out to sing to Farnsworth and give him his slop. Next, I took Agnes through her daily stenotype lesson, then retired to my kitchen to try to figure out how to make a cream sauce out of powdered skim milk and that margarine substitute beloved by Prudence Pennypincher called "spread."

After I had prepared the day's meals, I helped in the garden. There was something wrong with the garden but nobody knew what it was. I had my theories: Agnes treated it like a sickly child and so it became one, and then Polly intimidated it still further with her Department of Agriculture brochures. We tried commercial fertilizers but nothing helped. Finally, the postman suggested ordinary manure and gave Polly the name of a friend who kept horses. She called him and received a shock: he had all the manure she wanted, but he charged for it.

"Imagine!" she huffed. "He said why should he give away his manure when everybody in southern California was garden-crazy."

"That's exactly what you would say if you had a horse," I remarked.

She ignored me and drummed on the table in thought. After a moment, she looked up with a victorious glint in her eye.

"If we all ate nothing but raw vegetables for a week, we could produce manure ourselves."

"You can't be serious!" I burst out.

"Why not? It's self-sufficient, isn't it? Anything's better than *paying* for crap. Besides, with the weather as hot as it is, that's what we should be eating anyway. It'll be good for us."

We voted, and I lost. Gloria neither knew nor cared what she ate, and Agnes's experiences with bomb-shelter fare had destroyed her palate. Thus we resolved to buy vegetables at market prices, to make manure, to spread on our garden, so we wouldn't have to pay market prices for vegetables.

For chamber pots, we used the buckets that Uncle Ezra had used for his many street-corner fund drives; they all had SAVE THE WHALES painted on them. Polly handed them around, along with a set of very unnecessary instructions.

". . . and then empty it into the lidded garbage can I put beside the garden," she finished.

"We know how to crap, Polly." I sighed.

"And be sure to replace the lid."

I knew the reason for her long lecture. Given her chronic condition, she was trying to talk herself into making an equal contribution to the cause; undoubtedly she felt that if she *said* it often enough, she would *do* it. All the same, she made a quick trip to the drugstore for a large economy size box of Ultima Thules—just to be *sure*, as Agnes would say.

I did the best I could with the menus but everything tasted like what the diet books called "zesty." Polly banned mayonnaise from the kitchen—"Do horses eat Waldorf salad?"—so we ended up with the crudest of *crudités* and chewed so hard we drowned out the termites.

For the first two days I emptied my contribution quickly into the garbage can and left the area at once, but on the third day I succumbed to temptation. Surely, I thought, mine would look different from other people's. . . .

I fought my curiosity as long as I could; then I peeked. As soon as I did it I was too ashamed to notice much of anything. I replaced the lid and hurried up to my room to brood on the egotism of the only child.

That night as I sat at my window, I happened to look down just as Agnes scurried across the yard with her bucket. She opened the garbage can, but before she put anything in it, she raised her flashlight and peered in.

An hour or so later, Gloria emerged with her bucket. I had always thought her ego had fallen at Bannockburn but I was wrong: up came the lid and down went the flashlight for an inspection.

I ducked behind my curtain, turned off my light, and waited in the dark. I did not have to wait long. Soon I heard that unmistakable purposeful stride and suddenly there was the Great Equalizer herself, looking just like Diogenes as she studied the contents of the garbage can with a camper's lantern.

Self-love had triumphed over socialistic leveling, at least for the moment.

7

That's nothing compared to what I did for middle-aged women in 1937.

—Duchess of Windsor

Autumn came and Polly's mission began in earnest. She had vowed to fill the house with women and fill it she would, so she called another planning session to take a vote on her latest idea.

"The women who need the most help are those age fifty or over," she began. "Unskilled displaced home-makers whose husbands have deserted them. We're all young, so I think our next resident should be someone older. All in favor say aye."

Once again it was unanimous, though not for the self-less reasons Polly supposed. I said aye because I was used to old ladies. Agnes said it because she was too timid to disagree with Polly. As for Gloria, she simply enjoyed saying archaic words.

"Do you have somebody in mind?" I asked.

"Not yet, but I've contacted some Movement women in L.A. and they're going to find someone for us."

A few days later, she announced that a candidate for

our largesse had been found by none other than the nationally known feminist lawyer Samantha Banner.

"I've invited Samantha to dinner so she can tell us all the details about Martha Bailey. The woman is one of her clients."

That boded ill. Samantha Banner represented the kind of precision egalitarian who would settle for nothing less than an abortion performed by a gay black doctor under an endangered tree on a reservation for handicapped Indians. Her most famous case to date involved an effort to get the United States to break off diplomatic relations with France, Italy, Spain, and all other countries having a gender language. She herself was so radical she even objected to "Ms." She wanted to abolish all honorifics and call everybody "Person," abbreviated "Pn."

As six o'clock approached, I put the stroganoff in the warming oven and set up my cocktail bar. When everything was in readiness, we all sat down and waited for our renowned guest. Everyone looked very nice, even Gloria. In honor of the occasion she had refrained from curling her hair.

Soon we heard a car coming up the drive. Polly rose to go outside and do the honors. As she passed my chair, she leaned down and whispered a warning to me.

"Don't start any sentence with 'What this country needs is . . .' "

We all peered out the window for our first look at Samantha Banner in the flesh. To my surprise, she looked more like a suburban real estate saleswoman than a blood-throwing radical feminist. Tall, strong-looking, and fortyish, she had a gamine haircut and a deep bronze California tan. Instead of the usual pants-and-poncho Lib uniform she wore a timeless skirted suit with a jacket cut like a riding coat, a shoulder-strap bag, stacked heels, and driving gloves.

"Jésu!" Gloria exclaimed.

"What's the matter?"

She answered through clenched teeth. "School spirit!"

Never had those two honorable words been infused with so much venom. Never had Gloria displayed so much emotion either. Gone were the blurry smile and glassy eyes: she was seething. She simmered down before Samantha entered the living room but she continued to glower with barely suppressed hatred throughout dinner.

Before long I decided she had a point. It was easy to imagine Samantha Banner in college. She must have been one of those busy bees known as a "great girl," the kind with so many extracurricular activities that she throws the yearbook layout off. No doubt she had belonged to one of those great-girl honor societies with names like "Valkyries" whose chief goal was winning the basketball cup every year. And they won it, too; I could see Samantha's elbows at work. Great girls might serve on the honor council and never miss chapel, but they were entirely capable of throwing you down and sitting on your face if you crossed them. They made ideal radical feminists once they got their consciousnesses raised.

After dinner, Samantha opened her attaché case and took out a trial transcript.

"This will show you what poor Martha Bailey has been through," she said.

She was the type who handed out literature in living rooms and then sat back and waited for everybody to read it. Gloria folded her arms resolutely and continued to glower, so Polly, Agnes, and I did the honors.

The transcript said:

IN THE COUNTY OF LOS ANGELES $\Big\}$ ss.

IN THE STATE OF CALIFORNIA

Ms. Martha Bailey and "Regiment of Women, Inc." (a.k.a. "ROW")

Plaintiffs;

vs.

"Inflatable You" Lifesize Rubber Dolls, Inc.

Defendant.

For the Plaintiffs: MS. SAMANTHA BANNER

For the Defendant: MR. MACK LEE SLICK

MS. BANNER: Your Honor, the Plaintiffs contend that the product known as the Inflatable You Lifesize Rubber Doll, contrary to the manufacturer's claim that it is merely a party novelty, is intended solely for sexual use and furthermore, that it is degrading to women. We therefore ask that an injunction against its manufacture and sale be granted.

MS. MARTHA BAILEY, having first been duly sworn, testified as follows:

Q (by Ms. Banner): Ms. Bailey, are you the wife of Ronald Bailey?

A: I was for thirty years but he divorced me last year. He said I wasn't viable. I don't know what he meant by that. I've always washed carefully.

THE COURT: This is not a divorce hearing. Just answer the question.

Q: Ms. Bailey, please tell the court what happened on Saturday, July 27, 1971.

A: I was worried about Mr. Bailey living alone, so I made a batch of homemade scrapple and took it over to his apartment. He always liked my scrapple. I knocked several times but there was no answer, so I tried the door and it opened. I went in. And then I saw him. (Witness paused) On the bed.

Q: What was he doing?

A: He was having things to do with the rubber woman.

Q: Do you mean he was simulating sexual intercourse with the Inflatable You doll?

A: Yes.

Q: What did you do?

A: I got scared and threw the scrapple at them.

Q: What happened then?

A: The rubber woman blew up.

Q: What did your husband do?

A: He yelled for help. He was in pain. The rubber woman was wrapped around his private parts.

Q: Did you offer him assistance?

A: Yes.

Q: What did you do?

A: I pulled on it.

THE COURT: Order in the court.

Q: Were you able to get it off?

THE COURT: Order. Order. Order.

A: No.

Q: What happened then?

A: He had a heart attack.

Q: Ms. Bailey, I show you the remains of the rubber doll that was removed from your husband at the morgue. Is this what you saw on him?

A: Yes.

MS. BANNER: Your Honor, I request that this be marked and entered as Plaintiffs' Exhibit 1.

(The Exhibit, being a torn and shredded piece of flesh-colored latex and bearing two sections of what appeared to be hair or hair substitute on the head and pubic regions, and containing a facsimile of facial features as well as a partially dislodged mouthpiece and ripped air valve in the lumbar region, was marked and entered as Plaintiffs' Exhibit 1).

Q (by Ms. Banner): Ms. Bailey, I show you an advertisement from the magazine *Hung,* describing the item known as the Inflatable You Lifesize Rubber Doll, and ask you to read it into the record.

A: I can't, it's too dirty.

THE COURT: The Clerk will read it.

THE CLERK: Are you lonely? Do you want a girl who will obey your every wish and command? Then get acquainted with Dalilah, who never says no. Dalilah is five-feet-two inches tall and measures 44-23-35 from the top down, and Dalilah's top is always down.

THE COURT: Order in the court. If the spectators can't be serious they can leave. Bailiff, clear the courtroom.

(Whereupon, the courtroom was cleared)

THE COURT: The Clerk will continue the reading.

THE CLERK: Dalilah has real, authentic, lifelike features exact in every detail to a real live girl. Nothing is missing, and we mean nothing.

THE COURT: Bailiff, pull yourself together or get out. I'm warning you, Bailiff. All right, get out. We'll recess for fifteen minutes while I find a new bailiff.

(Whereupon, a fifteen-minute recess was called)

RESUMED

THE COURT: All right, Mr. Clerk, let's hear the rest of it.

THE CLERK: Dalilah loves to be dominated and will roll over at the snap of your fingers to try something new and different. She can take anything you can give, and best of all, she never stops smiling. Order her today. California residents please add five percent—

THE COURT: All right, never mind the rest.

MS. BANNER: We request that the ad be marked and entered, Your Honor.

(The Exhibit, being a piece of paper of the type known as pulp, bearing a black-and-white representation of said product and also reproduced photographs of said product lying on a bed beside a human male clad in a towel, and containing a perforated coupon, was marked and entered as Plaintiffs' Exhibit 2.)

MS. BANNER: Your Honor, I have here a new doll exactly like the one owned and used by Ms. Bailey's late husband. I ask the Court's permission to inflate it.

THE COURT: What is your purpose?

MS. BANNER: I would like to enter it, Your Honor.

THE COURT: Mr. Clerk, I will not tolerate levity from officials of this court. You are in contempt. Get out. I said get out. Bailiff, help him up and get him out of here.

(Whereupon the Clerk and the Bailiff left the courtroom.)

THE COURT: There is no need to blow it up, Ms. Banner, I grasp the principle. I'm going to dismiss this case. Leave this courtroom, Ms. Banner, and take that latex love goddess with you. Case dismissed.

(Whereupon, the Court was adjourned)

"So you see," said Samantha, when we had finished reading, "we met with mockery at every turn. I've filed an appeal but it will take a very long time. Meanwhile, Martha Bailey is terribly upset and very short of funds. Her husband named the doll, Dalilah, in his will, and now several real women named Dalilah have popped up to claim they knew him. Lies, of course, but it'll take forever to unsnarl."

"Martha Bailey needs all the supportiveness we can give her," said Polly, looking around at the rest of us. We nodded solemnly.

"Good," Samantha said briskly. "I'll bring her over tomorrow." With that, she picked up her transcript and left.

There was nothing to do but clear the table. Gloria, who had drawn K.P. duty on that week's RESPONSIBILITY SCHEDULE, got up and helped me, muttering imprecations as we made the long trek to the kitchen.

"Homecoming . . . student council . . . dormitory board . . . class picnic . . . we want to help you come out of your shell and make friends . . . I'd love to get my hands on your hair . . . rah-rah, siss-boom-bah, *shit, fuck, damn!*"

Suddenly, she threw herself to the floor and started baying at the moon.

"Gloria," I said when she had finished, "where are you from? You never told us."

"Iowa," she sighed. "I went to Iowa State." She picked herself up and snatched a dish towel from the rack. As we washed up, she told me her story.

"Those well-adjusted campus-leader types were always making fun of me. I *hate* sane people! That's why I decided to stick around with you and Polly—I could tell you were okay."

"I see."

The next morning, Samantha drove out with Martha Bailey.

Even before she uttered the identifying "How do?" I sensed she was a Southerner. Not a Virginia Piscop or a Maryland Catholic or a Charleston Shintoist but a down-home Baptist, with a blond Jesus on her calendars and relatives in Folsom Prison.

She looked like Ma Joad but without the iron, stout and frumpish, with blue-rinsed hair crimped into finger waves. As she shook hands with us her self-effacement was almost tangible. I imagined her putting slipcovers on furniture and then throw covers over the slipcovers in a symbolic attempt to hide herself. She was the woman destroyed by one good ole boy too many.

She relaxed a little after Samantha left, but when she found out I was a writer she gave me a look of dread like a silent scream and launched into a disjointed warning.

"I don't see how you can stand it. All that mental concentration would make me nervous. Don't it make you nervous? I have to do somethin' with my hands. It gentles me, don't you know? Seems to me like writin' books would be mighty bad on the nerves. You'd be better off if you tried to keep busy. It don't do to think too hard.

Keep the mind free and the hands busy, I always say."

It was Granny all over again, but with an important difference: Martha identified with me. When she had gone upstairs to her room, I took Polly aside for a private word.

"She's having the change of life."

"The *menopause*," she corrected.

"But don't you see what she's doing? She's afraid of cracking up, so she's trying to deny it by pinning the rose on me."

"What rose?"

I elaborated on my theory and got a left-handed compliment for my pains.

"Projection? Never heard of it. You're always inventing things. The menopause," she said authoritatively, "is a natural phase in woman's cycle of growth. We need to throw off these annotated fears and think of it as a new and exciting adventure. If Martha is afraid of the menopause it's because she's been culturally conditioned to fear it. It's not her fault."

"I didn't say it was."

"No, but you tend to see everything in terms of the *individual*." Her nose quivered on certain key words and that was one of them. "You have to look for the root societal cause."

I was left alone with my annotated fears.

As luck would have it, I had just returned to writing after my summer block. This time I was trying my hand at a Gothic in hopes that living in Uncle Ezra's windswept house would inspire me.

I hated Gothics even more than Regencys so it was hard going but I had to *keep* going because of Martha. As long as she heard the typewriter she didn't worry, but whenever it fell silent for any length of time she would rush upstairs to see if I had committed suicide. As I sat hunched over my desk in thought, I would hear a little scuffle and look up to see her worried bifocaled eyes peering at me from the doorway.

Overnight, I changed from a blocked writer to the Thompson gun of literature. To keep her away from me, I started writing anything I could think of as fast as I could type it, ending up with such models of structure as: "Sir Giles hid the missing Will in Farmer Tankard's well as Lady Henrietta was returning from a mysterious visit to the vicarage when lightning struck her landaulet as Mrs. Braithewaite the evil housekeeper watched from the tower with a menacing laugh which sent a chill up my spine while Hawkins lit the tapers that made the dog howl and scurry under the settee where he ate the crumpled letter dropped by the gamekeeper before I could read it."

This was another version of writing block called "putting words on paper." When I finally ran down, my fingers were numb and tingling—a sure sign of the menopause—and furthermore, I felt strangely hot. I got up to open the window, but that didn't do my nerves any good at all because I found Martha on the veranda.

With immense casualness, and no doubt telling herself: *Act natural with 'em just like they was anybody else,* she cast around for something nonchalant to say to a writer.

"You like Shakespeare?"

"Yes, my favorite play is *Timon of Athens.* It's about a man who had 'go away' carved on his tombstone."

"I heard you goin' lickety-split at the typewriter just now," she said worriedly. "You know, honey, it don't do to hurry. It can get you all worked up. I used to know somebody who was always hurryin' and she just up and went to pieces one day. Just like that!" she warned, snapping her fingers. Her voice dropped to a dramatic whisper. "They had to put her away."

She gave me a hang-in-there wink and left. I sank

down in a chair and put my head in my hands. Now I was damned if I typed and damned if I didn't. I had to get away.

I decided to buy Polly another pig, and take Farnsworth and Quadrupet and go. That would mean buying a car, or more probably a pickup truck, and getting some sort of livestock-transport license, all traumatic events for someone who wanted to sit alone in a room and write. My agoraphobia had gotten worse since moving to California, the Outdoors State. I dreaded going to one of their huge, endless car lots and being swarmed over by men in coonskin caps trying to give me free hot dogs. Equally upsetting was the thought of roaming through the endless corridors of bureaucracy explaining to strangers my reasons for wanting to take a pig to New Orleans.

That was another problem: New Orleans. I was perfectly willing to spend the rest of my life in a studio apartment overtop a grocery store and across the street from a post office, but where would I put Farnsworth? I would have to live in some isolated rural spot, which meant more agoraphobia.

It was a no-win situation. I was still mulling it over two days later when Samantha telephoned with her bright idea.

"I want to appeal to the state legislators through their stomachs," she told Polly. "Martha's pièce de résistance is scrapple. If she would bake a small scrapple loaf for each member of the Legislature, I could hit them with my anti-porn petition, which in turn would help Martha win her rubber doll suit. ROW will pay for the scrapple ingredients and we'll use your van to deliver the gifts to Sacramento. What do you say?"

"Beautiful!" Polly said.

I didn't move in time, so I got involved in the scrapple campaign. It began with the usual feminist powwow about what to call it.

"Loafs for Legislators!" Polly suggested brightly.

"Loaves," I corrected, heaving a great sigh. "As in fishes."

"She's right, Polly," said Martha, with raised eyebrows and a series of quick little signaling nods. I could hear her telling herself: *It's best not to contradict 'em.*

After settling on the name, our next task was PROCUREMENT. Translated from the Polly it meant driving miles out in the country to a farm where we bought ears, snouts, hocks, lungs, sow belly, and other cheap porcine parts. These would be boiled together with livers, kidneys, brains, and a ham bone until they reached the consistency of an acid-bath-murder victim, then ground up and mixed with corn meal and formed into Loafs for Loafers.

The procurement trip upset me. I loved scrapple but I loved Farnsworth more. That night I had terrible dreams in which Polly, to save money, slaughtered Farnsworth and served me a pudding made of his blood and bones, and I, like Queen Tamora in *Titus Andronicus,* ate it without knowing that it was my child.

Scrapple Day dawned sunny and bright, like every other goddamn day. We all gathered in the kitchen to contribute our services. Martha issued each of us a thick-webbed black triangular hairnet, explaining in hushed tones that men always got mad when they found hair in their food, and showed us how to tie them on in the professional cook manner.

The style emphasized Polly's chiseled facial bones and made her look like the Hollywood version of a young nun who has just removed her wimple without realizing that a captivated Peter Finch is standing behind her. Agnes simply looked like Agnes in a hairnet, and Gloria actually looked better. I looked like the torpedo in *The Enemy Below.*

The production began, and with it Polly's hoof-in-mouth disease.

"Tell us what you want us to do, Martha," she said timidly. "You're in charge here."

Her attempt at flattery came through loud and thick. Instant dominance was too much for Martha. Thus far she had been relaxed and ready to have some girlish fun, but now she grew red and flustered under the staggering blow of Polly's tact.

She reached nervously for her apron, a frilly affair with a bib, and put it on over the tank top and jeans she had been wearing since falling into ROW's hands. The contrast had all the melancholy of Emily Dickinson's certain slant of light. I glanced at Polly to see if she had noticed it, but she was standing nobly at parade rest awaiting orders.

"You three can chop," Martha said, handing cleavers to Polly, Agnes, and Gloria. Naturally she would not let me near such a dangerous tool. I was given the elevating task of denuding snouts of stray hairs.

When the meat was chopped and ready, the boiling began. We used Martha's preserving kettle, which she had brought with her when she moved in with us, and the biggest pots and pans in the house. Soon there was no more room on the stove, so we hunted up some old hotplates. A small state with a unicameral legislature would have been hard enough to seduce, but we were cooking for California.

The whole house reeked of swine, and as the official stirrer—I had been issued a harmless wooden spoon—I got the worst of it. Martha's scrapple was delicious in finished form but in the deliquescing stage it was unbearable. Worse than the smell was the way it looked. Every time I gave it a stir I brought up something that reminded me of Farnsworth: his little cloven hooves, his retroussé snout, his fatty but loving heart.

When the first batch was melted, I gave it to the other three helpers, who cut out the gristle and gave it to Martha.

"Now comes the hard part," she said proudly. "You have to push it through a sieve. You girls watch and I'll show you how to do it."

That's when Polly opened her big mouth.

"You don't have to go to all that trouble," she said airily. "There's no point in doing it the old-fashioned way when we have two blenders and a food mill."

Martha's face crumpled like the pig flesh just before it came loose from the bone. She wept soundlessly at first, her tears indistinguishable from the sweat drops on her cheeks. Then she gave a loud choking sob and ran from the kitchen. It was an old lady's run that was enough to break the heart.

Polly, of course, looked dumbfounded. "What did I say?"

Martha was stumbling from room to room, shrieking, sobbing, and stuffing her knuckles into her mouth. We all ran after her, with Polly babbling as only Polly could.

"I'll drive you to the Crisis Center. You'll feel better there, everybody's upset at the Crisis Center. You can have a dialogue with somebody who's in same-stage restructuring. They have a new group called the Feisty Fifties for displaced homemakers. You can get everything out of your system in an atmosphere of sharing. They've just instituted a lecture series on aspects of transitional—"

"SHUT UP!" Gloria bellowed.

Agnes jumped and said "Oh, mercy!" and Polly shut up.

As we watched in amazement, Gloria sat down on Martha's generous lap and put her arms around her neck. As they rocked back and forth it was impossible to tell who was comforting whom or which was the dominant figure. Gloria pulled her T-shirt out of her valance line and wiped Martha's eyes, then helped her upstairs.

She returned a few moments later. "I gave her a Valium," she said. "It'll knock her out."

"Gloria," Polly warned reproachfully, "unprescribed drugs are very dangerous. Martha needs professional—"
"EEEEEEEEOOOOOOOOOWWWWWWWWWW!" Gloria replied.

It was the most bloodcurdling ululation I had ever heard, in or out of movies. Rolling her eyes back until nothing showed but the whites, she squatted on the floor, stuck her thumbs in her ears, and waggled her fingers at us.

"Sanity, sanity, all is sanity! *Fuck* professional help! *Fuck* centers! *Fuck* clinics! FUCK! FUCK! FUCK!"

Before Polly could comment, an explosive sizzle came from the kitchen, followed by a malodorous waft of singed flesh.

"The pots are boiling over!"

We ran to the rescue but it was too late. The kitchen looked like Russia under Ivan the Terrible. I peered into the preserving kettle and recoiled: an ear floating on the surface of the water was swelling up in rhythmic blisters from the turmoil raging underneath. I grabbed a knife and stabbed it to let the air through and it exploded with such force that I thought I'd been shot. I pushed it to the bottom of the pot but a reeking kidney took its place. The smell of steaming urine made me so sick that I threw up in the sink. By the time I got the sink washed, the ear was back.

"What're we going to do with all this stuff?" Agnes cried. "We can't manage without Martha."

"Don't worry," Polly said officiously. "We can finish it. All we have to do is follow the recipe."

"There isn't any," I said. "Martha cooks without recipes. It's one of those old-fashioned talents that gives her what little self-esteem she has."

I grabbed my wooden paddle and pulled it through the thickening mixture. "We've got to do something before this shit turns to soap!"

I said it in a spirit of hysterical masochism, knowing

that it would be just like Polly to pick this moment, of all times, to point out that soap requires ashes. If she did, I planned to hit her with the paddle, providing I could get it out of the pot.

"Cornmeal!" she said brightly. "I remember now! She said you're supposed to mix the meat with cornmeal."

Before anyone could stop her, she grabbed a huge sack of cornmeal and dumped its contents into the pots. Now the pig mixture began to swell and heave and give off a silvery scum like snail droppings. We panicked and added water to cool it down, but we added too much, so we had to pour in some more cornmeal to thicken it. When it threatened to harden into cement, we added more water, promptly causing what Polly called "a lack of consistency," a situation we corrected by adding more cornmeal.

We ended up with something that would have turned even a politician's stomach. Everybody collapsed at the kitchen table and tried to figure out what to do.

"Now I know what the Bible means by a mess of pottage." Agnes sighed.

"It's inedible," I said. "It looks like an oil slick with lumps. We'll have to throw it out."

Polly's eyes nearly popped out of her head. "We can't! We'd be out of pocket! We'd have to pay ROW back if we threw it away, so we'll have to find a use for it." She pursed her lips. "Waste not, want not."

"The Lord giveth and the Lord taketh away. Tell him to come and get it." I put my head down on the table and burped.

"It's perfectly good food with lots of nutritious ingredients," she argued. "Somebody would be thankful for it."

"We could donate it to that church we saw in town," Agnes suggested. "You know—the one without a steeple?"

"That's a synagogue."

"Oh. . . ." She thought a moment, then brightened. "I know! We can give it to Farnsworth!"

"He wouldn't eat himself!" I cried, horrified.

We argued over the old adage that pigs will eat anything but none of us knew the answer. Punch-drunk from strain and fatigue, Gloria and I got knottily philosophical, with me defending Farnsworth's ethics like an early church father clinging to a point of doctrine while she played the devil's advocate, trying to destroy me via the Socratic method.

It was too much for Polly. "Never mind that stuff! *I* know what we can do. We'll donate it to the battered wife shelter in Ventura. That way," she said happily, "ROW will still be willing to foot the bill and we won't have to reimburse them."

"Okay," I sighed, too tired to argue with her. "Internal injuries are internal injuries."

"You can tell them it's suet pudding," Gloria said dryly.

Having decided how to get rid of it, we promptly got into another argument about how to transport it.

"We can't take it in the pots; we won't have anything left to cook in," I said. "We'll have to put it all in one big container."

"We don't have anything that big," Polly countered.

"Yes, we do. The birth bucket."

"No!" she cried, the tigress protecting her young.

"We don't have any choice."

She finally relented and we committed the sacrilege. I held my breath as the porcine glue hit the bottom of the bucket with a splat. Agnes elected to stay behind in case Gloria needed help with Martha, so Polly and I lugged the necrotic donation out to the van and shoved it in.

"One of us will have to sit in back and steady it so it won't tip over," Polly said.

There was no doubt about who the one would be; ever since the U-Haul incident I had refused to drive the van. I crawled into the stygian gloom of the cargo section and put my arms around our vat of witches' brew.

The Ventura battered wife shelter was on top of a steep hill in an old clapboard house in the center of town. Polly, who knew the keeper, bounced in and announced in cheery tones, "We have a special treat for you!" Then she returned to help me get it inside.

It was like trying to move the Rock of Behistun. The situation demanded what worried generals call "upper body strength" when arguing against women in combat, but we didn't have any after all the hours we had spent stirring piggy concrete. Add to that the fact that despite my heroic efforts to steady it while the van was in motion, some of the scrapple soup had slopped over to form a greasy residue on the handles. Does it come as any surprise that we dropped the birth bucket?

If only it had broken, everything would have ended simply, but it didn't. As we watched in horror, it tipped over on its side and started rolling down the hill.

"Catch it!" Polly yelled, a déjà vu trigger by now, and off we went behind it.

A rolling birth bucket gathers no moss. People saw it coming and jumped clear, giving it a perfect, unobstructed path all the way to the bottom, where it glanced off the curb and smashed to bits against a car with a blue light on its roof.

We arrived, breathless, and saying things like "Oh, God, the birth bucket!" The cops inside the squad car rose from their hunched positions, surveyed the muck-filled dents in their hood, and then looked out the window at us. We were both dressed in our oldest work clothes; I in ragged jeans and sweatshirt and Polly in railroad engineer's striped overalls with a big *ERA—NOW* button pinned on the bib.

The cops got out and walked toward us in that slow, ponderous gait of cops getting ready to be cops. One of them reached for his notebook and spoke.

"Well, girls, what've we got here?"

"*Women!*" Polly barked. I closed my eyes.

He pushed back his cap and chewed on the side of his lip, his glance flickering over her button.

"Uh-huh," he said. He must have had the best *uh-huh* in the law enforcement business; there was nothing on television to match it. Looking down at his shoe, he studied the glob of grease on his toe as though it were a priceless objet d'art and he a leisurely collector who never hurried.

At last he bent down and picked up a gleaming white object. "What kinda bone is this?" he demanded.

"I refuse to answer!"

"It's a ham bone," I said placatingly.

She snapped her head around to me. "Don't weaken!"

Next he picked up something that looked like a transparent rubber handkerchief. It was the ear.

"What kinda skin is this?"

Suddenly I remembered from my detective story reading that human flesh looks almost exactly like fresh pork.

"It's a pig's ear," I said helpfully. "We were making scrapple and—"

"We refuse to answer any questions until you read us our Miranda!"

"Miranda, huh?" said the cop, smiling an enigmatic smile. "*Ho*-kay. If the *women* want their Miranda, they'll get their Miranda. One for each." He reached into his pocket and handed us plastic cards.

"That's very nice," I said hurriedly, handing mine back.

"Wait," said Polly. "You have to *read* it to us."

I tried to jab her in the ribs but all I did was hurt my

elbow. She had gone as stiff as a board from righteous wrath. The cop cleared his throat theatrically and rattled off the caution from memory, then signaled to his partner.

"We gotta have this *alleged* pork substance analyzed by the lab. If you *women* will be good enough to accompany us to headquarters—"

"COSSACK!"

"That does it! In the car, *women!*"

"Jack, the effin' car won't start," said the driver. "They must've busted somethin' with that depth charge."

"No problem," the first cop said airily. "It's such a lovely day, we'll walk. That'll give us the pleasure of escorting two lovely *women.* Right this way, *women.*"

It was only two blocks to police headquarters but that was plenty of time for six choruses of so simple a song as "We Shall Overcome." I tried to get Polly's attention to make her shut up but it was impossible. She was walking in front with her cop and I was behind her with mine. It looked like a double date; both of them were swinging plastic sample bags full of scrapple as though we were on our way to a picnic.

When we came to headquarters, Polly suddenly collapsed. Innocent that I was in the techniques of protest, I thought she had fainted, but I was wrong.

"GO LIMP! GO LIMP!" she yelled at me.

If I had, there would have been nobody to catch me. They were all struggling with her. Another policeman came out of the building to help her in. She was so limp that her arms and legs were draped around their shoulders like sleeping pythons. Ignored by all, I held my head up high and walked unaided into the station house. At the door, I accidentally bumped into yet another cop and said "Excuse me" just like Marie Antoinette when she stepped on the guillotiner's toe.

* * *

We were released an hour later after an obviously mock laboratory analysis of our scrapple.

"Fascists!" Polly ground out, as we left the building. "I'll sue them for false arrest!"

"It was your fault."

"*My* fault! You didn't say a word! I did all the talking! *I* was the one who defended our rights!"

"Is that the way you see it? Do you actually think that's what happened?"

"Think? I don't think, I *know!*"

As the cop said, that did it. "Your mouth ought to be bronzed!" I exploded. "Then we could put it up on a shelf and everybody could look at it and say, 'There was a mouth! Shall we ever see another?' This whole *day* happened because of your mouth! It started when you delivered the coup de grace to Martha!"

She frowned pensively. "The what?"

"Oh, *God!*"

We maintained a stony silence on the drive back. When we got home, I fed Farnsworth, took a shower, and went to bed with Quadrupet snuggled under my chin.

To my astonishment, a contrite Polly brought me a cup of coffee the next morning.

"Would you like a natural egg?" she asked nervously.

"No. Leave us alone."

It went on like that for several more days. I had never known her to be so anxious to make amends. Until now, her guilt had manifested itself along grandiose liberal lines like worrying about entire countries, but now she was dumping ashes on her head in honor of one, single, solitary individual whom she actually knew.

She even went so far as to *buy* a paperback called *How to Develop a Sense of Humor,* with worksheets in the back. She saw nothing remotely funny about that—to Polly it was evidence of a serious program of study—but she chuckled mightily over the author's examples of his own wit, such as: "When my son said his English class was reading *David Copperfield*, I said, 'what the dickens!' and we all had a good laugh."

When I told her that the son probably went around in a perpetual cringe saying, "Jeez, Dad, cut it out, will you?" she glared at me and told me I was an élitist.

We were back to normal.

8

Sometimes occasions occur in life from whence you have to be slightly mad in order to extricate yourself.
                                              —La Rochefoucauld

Nothing can cure raging hormonal imbalance like raging imbalance. By some mysterious therapeutic method, Gloria put Martha back together again in a matter of weeks.

Everybody had a different theory about it. Polly said it was inborn sisterhood, which she believed was spontaneous, like combustion, and sentimental Agnes decided that Martha must have had a daughter who died, and now Gloria had taken her place and given her someone to live for.

I felt that Gloria's Middle English drivelations, which drove everybody else crazy, had driven Martha sane. Hailing as she did from the linguistically frozen Smoky Mountains, where people still used words like "gainsay," meeting a girl of twenty-three who called epilepsy the "fallyng sickness" had put her menopause in perspective and made age a matter of the utmost relativity.

"I don't see what that has to do with anything," said Polly after I had finished theorizing.

"Oh, never mind," I sighed.

L'affaire scrapple was a turning point for the Don't Tread on Me Women's Commune. We entered one of those curious limbos of pleasant dullness that men have in mind when they say, "All I want is a little peace and quiet." Agnes and Martha did each other's hair, Gloria spent her time constructing a dulcimer, and I practiced my specialty, doing crossword puzzles in ink.

Polly, of course, kept stoking the eternal flame, but nothing penetrated our complacency. She tried to turn dinner into a consciousness-raising session, but the moment she said, "The vagina is a hated Other," Martha doused it with, "I don't think we should talk about our private parts at the table."

After-dinner discussions on *Wholeness in the Restructured Workplace* sank in a sea of pink-collar hysteria when Agnes swallowed a bobby pin. The air was pungent with permanent-waving lotion and despairing cries of "I can't get this even!" from Gloria. She meant her F-sharp hammer, but it sounded like home sewing. We had turned into a sorority house.

Naturally it couldn't last. The spell was broken by Samantha Banner, who dropped by one day to see, of all people, me.

"ROW needs some help with our literary quarterly. How would you like to be editor of *The Enchanted Clitoris?*"

I glanced at Polly, wondering if she had put her up to it.

"It would only take you two or three days' work every three months," she pleaded prettily. "You could pick any days that suit you, or simply come in with Polly when she does her volunteer work for us. That way you wouldn't have to make a special trip. I hope you can help us, Isabel. *The Enchanted Clitoris* needs your touch."

She had no idea what my touch was—it had been

carefully kept from her—but in one sense she was right. I was powerless to stop the promulgation of ROW's madcap theories, but at least I could stop them from gang-raping the English language.

ROW's house organ was the *cloaca maxima* of the written word, a jargon-soaked collection of philippics by fulminating feminists whose first rule was: "Don't worry about grammar or spelling, just let it come." What spewed forth were loonynyms like "the clink in Sam Erwin's armor," dummynyms like "I see a cataract in the desert," and the most glorious homonyms since *"tante pis."*

Reading any feminist prose made me weep for Shakespeare and Austen; when I read *The Enchanted Clitoris* I wept for Zane Grey and Olive Higgins Prouty.

"Okay, I'll do it."

"I think that's *fine,*" Polly said stoutly.

ROW's storefront headquarters was full of women in rimless glasses who all looked as if they were saving a seat for Madame de Farge. The atmosphere was sweetened only by the aroma of freshly sawed lumber that emanated from the endless rows of makeshift pamphlet shelves that lined every wall.

Polly led the way down a long corridor past the assertiveness-training class, from which bloodcurdling screams of "This steak is tough!" and "I demand to see the manager!" poured forth like a perpetual litany from a demented abbey.

We entered Samantha's office and found her on the phone. She motioned us to sit down and put her hand over the mouthpiece. "It's our New York office!" she hissed importantly, and then returned to her conversation.

"I believe we can hit them with a child-abuse suit. I've read everything they've published in the child-possession line: *Damon the Demon, Owen the Omen,* and *The Bergering*—that's the one about the little bar mitzvah boy. They're definitely in a conspiracy to denigrate children. I'll write the brief tonight. Meanwhile, you take your group down there and throw blood on them."

She hung up and gave us a triumphant smile. "I've directed our Free Speech Committee to invade the editorial offices of Alger House. They've just come out with a novel called *Umbilicus Rex* about a fetus who chews up his father's penis during intercourse."

"That's good for a six-figure paperback sale," I said.

Samantha's eyes stretched open so wide I experienced an overpowering need to squeeze mine shut. It was the visual counterpart to hearing fingernails rake down a blackboard.

"You're so right!" she said intensely, giving me a look of new respect. "I'm glad to hear a professional writer condemn it."

Misunderstood as usual.

Polly went off to her committee and Samantha led me to my desk. A towering stack of submissions in brown manuscript envelopes covered most of the working surface.

"Polly said you worked on your college literary magazine, so you know what a dummy is."

"Yes."

"Well, then, you won't have any trouble. All you have to do is type up any handwritten submissions, paste up the dummy, and send it to the All About Lilith Press. Here's their address," she said, pulling a business card from the corner of the calendar.

I went through the drawers and found the necessary tools of the editorial trade: ruler, blue pencils, and cropping wheel. There was only one thing missing.

"Where are the rejection slips?"

Samantha's eyes stretched open again. I turned my head and relieved myself with a quick blink.

"We don't have any," she replied. "We never reject anything. That would imply that some people can write and others can't."

"But suppose it's no good?"

I thought her forehead was going to split open this time.

"That's a value judgment," she said reprovingly.

"But suppose it makes no sense? Like the ramblings of a demented mind, for instance?"

"Dementia is relative. Besides, our readers could learn much from the inner thoughts of the mentally disturbed."

I couldn't argue with that, but neither could I take in the idea of a magazine that accepted the entire slush pile. I tried another angle.

"Suppose somebody submits something that has nothing to do with feminism?"

She gave me a sublime smile. "Everything has something to do with feminism."

I wondered how she felt about the War of Jenkins' Ear. After she returned to her office I skimmed through a copy of the latest issue. The logo of *The Enchanted Clitoris* was exactly what you would expect it to be; there was a big one on the cover and lots of little ones scattered through the text. They were used after each page number and at the end of each article to signify *The End*, like *Cosmopolitan*'s pussycat.

Most of the text consisted of the letters column called "Vent-a-Spleen," which took up twelve pages. In addition, there was a poetry section, a female rage section, a fiction section for children, called "Freewheelers," and a regular feature called "My Most Unforgettable Bisexual."

There were even a few carefully chosen ads. No vibrator shaped like a penis could be shown, but shower attachments were acceptable, and so were ads for an oval hand vibrator that ran on transistor batteries and looked like a horse groomer's curry comb. Polly had one but she used it to wax furniture.

I found my favorite ad, which appeared in every issue in the same place of honor on the inside front cover.

Do you have trouble getting through to people? Do people have trouble getting through to you? If so, you need PERCEPTO-PHONE! A record a day will help you develop insight in 12 easy lessons! Only $16.95! Order now! (stereo console not included).

I looked with dismay at the mountain of copy on my desk. Given ROW's editorial policy, it would take five years to use it all. I felt like the bird that tried to fill the ocean with one grain of sand at a time.

I opened the biggest envelope first, figuring somebody had sent us a novel, but it turned out to he a sample marriage contract worthy of a Wittelsbach princess and a Hohenzollern margrave. I hid it in the bottom drawer and started on the letters.

Most of them were some version of "I'm proud to be a Lesbian! (Name withheld)." I finally found one that was signed, but the signature was the only thing that made any sense. The body of the letter was a vertiginous shower of ellipses interspersed with words—an attempted simulation of the Sapphic fragment by a Lesbian who Grecianized her girlfriend's name: "The night we ... oneness ... wetness ... Bettyis."

I found an article called "Pistol Packin' Prostate" that was suitable for the female rage section as far as the content was concerned. As far as the syntax was concerned it was a pluperfect mess. The writer had failed to start her narrative far enough back in time, causing the entire piece to read like a double flashback:

"I had had an orgasm when I had slept with him the second time, but I had not known it had happened, since

I had had no experience other than the affair I had had during the summer I had spent in Nepal."

I picked up a pencil and started to fix it, but just then Samantha appeared in the doorway and stopped me.

"Wait. You mustn't change anything."

"But it's an awkward sentence."

"That's a value judgment. *The Enchanted Clitoris* is a journal of individual expression."

"Can't I even correct bad grammar?"

"There's no such thing. Everyone has a right to his or her own English. To insist upon rules is élitist," she ruled. "Underprivileged people, for example, do marvelous things with nontraditional grammar."

She was wrong. Only the horsey set can make bad grammar attractive. It takes generations of money and breeding to infuse "he don't" with élan.

"If you correct someone else's writing, you set up a structured relationship," she went on. "Remember ROW's motto: Nobody on Top."

I had a fleeting fantasy of Samantha screwing on her side, with her strong, basketball player's leg flung over some poor little milky-white male hip.

Suddenly she snapped her fingers and hit herself on the forehead. "Oh, I almost forgot! There's something terribly important that has to get in this issue."

She hurried back to her office and returned with a sheet of paper. She handed it to me with a flourish.

"It's my report on publishers of pornographic books in Los Angeles," she said proudly. "I'm going to expose them. See? I've listed their names, addresses, phone numbers, and pay scales."

"I see."

"None of this information is available in *Writer's Market.*"

"I know."

"I interviewed one of the authors. Do you know what

he told me? The books have no plots and no characterization, so it's possible to write one in a week. He did
two a week and made a fortune. Isn't it awful that they
pay so much for such anti-woman filth?"

"Yes." I wished she'd shut up; I was trying to read.

"I can't imagine how anyone could write it, can you?"

"No."

"Make sure you run it in a prominent place."

I looked up and gave her a dedicated smile. "I'll mark
it *Must Go.*"

When she left, I took my memo book from my bag and
copied all the names and addresses. When lunchtime
came, I invented a trip to the public library and grabbed
a taxi.

The highest-paying porn publisher on Samantha's list
was Sword & Scabbard, located in a small office building
on Sunset Boulevard between a massage parlor and the
United Gnostic Church of the People.

I entered the lobby and looked at the neat, glassed-in
bulletin board. Except for Sword & Scabbard, the tenants
sounded eminently conventional. There was a PR outfit,
an insurance salesman, a draftsman, and the representative of a crop-dusting company. The only one that worried me was a man who called himself an oral surgeon,
but when I got upstairs and smelled Lavoris I knew he
was a real dentist.

I found Sword & Scabbard's office and opened the
door. A girl who appeared to be a receptionist looked up
from her desk. She was putting something into her
mouth but it was only a doughnut. It made her look like
any receptionist anywhere. I relaxed a little and returned
her lumpy smile.

I told her I was a writer and asked Iif I could have a
word with one of the editors.

"You mean Amy? Just a minute, I'll call and see."

While she was on the intercom, I tried to imagine a porn editor named Amy. It made me think of girls who cried on their wedding nights. I decided she must be one of the new breed of soybean Amys who take natural names along with natural food. Those people had a lot of Mauds, too.

In a moment, Amy emerged from the inner office. I couldn't believe my eyes; she was a natural honey blonde who didn't look a day over eighteen. When she came closer I saw that she was in her late twenties, but otherwise she was the incarnation of State Fair.

"Hi," she said with a pleasant smile. "I'm Amy Chandler. Come on back to my office."

She wore a pair of burgundy slacks with a matching tunic. No chains, no American flags in unpatriotic places, and no buttons except the ones that held her clothes together. It was too good to be true; the place must be a front for something even worse than a porn publisher.

Her office looked like every editor's office I had ever seen: manuscripts in brown envelopes piled in a corner, galleys trailing over the desk like giant tapeworms, and an unfinished letter in the typewriter. The girlish touches recommended by *Cosmopolitan* were also in evidence: plants, a big brandy snifter full of hard candy, a piggy bank, and a quill ballpoint stuck in a Styrofoam snowball.

The most incredible touch of all was a white rabbit in a hutch.

"This is Mac," Amy said, poking a finger through his cage to give him a scratch. "He's our mascot."

He looked like a herbivorous Quadrupet. I sat down and told Amy about my writing experience.

"Oh, gee!" she exclaimed. "You've written *real* books."

"Regencys?" I said, stunned.

"It's all in what you're used to," she said philosophically. "To me, a Regency is a real book after this." She picked up one of the galleys with the tips of her finger and immediately dropped it with a shudder.

"How long have you worked here?"

"Almost a year." She put an index finger to her temple and pulled an imaginary trigger. "I came to California to start a boutique but it went broke. I had to do something so . . ." She gestured at the four walls of her office.

"Where are you from?"

"Terre Haute, Indiana."

A porn editor from the banks of the Wabash.

Suddenly the door opened and a man came in. I whirled around, expecting to die. *He had something in his hand!*

It was a Thom McAn shoebox full of cookies.

"Hi," he said, offering the box. "Have one. My wife made them."

The medieval world had Everyman; America has Every-husband. He was it. I took a cookie and Amy introduced us.

"Isabel, this is our editor in chief, Bill Wheeler. Isabel wants to write for us."

"Oh, gosh, that's great. Glad to have you aboard."

What was going on? Amy, gosh, gee, Indiana, rabbits, homemade cookies, and a Navy vet named Bill who shopped at Thom McAn. Instead of a den of iniquity, it was Waspville, U.S.A.

"Who owns Sword & Scabbard?" I asked suddenly.

"God only knows," Bill said. "I can't afford to care. I came out here from Joplin, Missouri to work for a big ad agency. Everything was hunky-dory for about a year; then they played musical chairs and I lost. I had to do something, so . . ." He gestured at the walls the way Amy had.

We got down to business—that wonderful editorial subject known as "needs." Writers never ask editors questions, we "query" them, and instead of saying "What do you want?" we always say "What are your needs?" With magazine editors, it's "current needs."

"Dirt," said Amy. "Two hundred double-spaced pages of it. Here are some samples of the kind of thing we publish." She handed me two Sword & Scabbard paperbacks. One was called *Dipstick* and the other *Swallowing It.*

"And here," she continued, rummaging in her desk, "is a copy of our editorial guidelines. I don't know if it'll do you any good or not. It was written by a guy who used to work here and he was pretty weird, but you might as well take it along."

"The most important thing to remember is not to try anything fancy, like telling a story," Bill advised. He pointed to a framed quotation on the wall above Mac's cage. "Remember what Sir Francis Bacon said."

I got up and read it. It was from the *Essays.* "Some books are to be tasted, others are to be swallowed, and some few to be chewed and digested." Beneath the quotation someone had written: "Ours are to be jerked off."

"And thereby hangs a tail," said Amy.

"Just keep that in mind and you'll be all right," said Bill. "Let's see . . . what are some of our other taboos?"

"Humor," said Amy. "For gosh sakes, don't write anything funny, whatever you do. Humor destroys eroticism. Besides, a lot of our readers are real psychos—they might think you were laughing at *them.*" She fanned herself with her fingers.

"Marriage is another taboo," Bill said. "Nobody's ever married in our books."

"Pregnancy is out, too," Amy said. "Let the reader assume that all the women characters are on the Pill, but don't *mention* the Pill or any other form of birth control. Porn readers don't like women who think ahead. They take it personally."

"And don't give any of the characters ethnic names," Bill cautioned. "Make everybody a Wasp. That way, nobody will get insulted."

I stuffed the guidelines and the sample copies into my

tote bag and rose. Like the well-brought-up people they were, Amy and Bill walked me to the door. When we got to the outer office they introduced me to the receptionist.

"Isabel, meet Mary Beth Cartwright. Isabel's going to write for us."

"Oh, golly, that's terrific!" exclaimed Mary Beth, and then she, too, got up to walk me to the door. I noticed that she had a limp.

"I used to be a ballet student," she explained, "but then I lost two toes in a snowmobile accident when I went home to Wisconsin last Christmas. That was the end of my ballet career. I had to do something, so . . ."

She made the Sword & Scabbard gesture and took a cookie from Bill's box. "Ummm, these are even better than my mom's."

We lingered at the door and talked some more in good small-town fashion. When I finally left, Bill called out a last-minute piece of encouragement.

"Just keep it simple and you'll have it in the barn before you know it."

Whoever owned Sword & Scabbard, at least there was one corner of a foreign field that would forever be the North 40.

In the cab back to ROW, I studied *Guidelines for Our Authors.* They sounded as if they had been written by a vice-squad detective who was taking a course in the elegiac couplet at an unaccredited night school.

1. To lessen readers' confusion, kindly avoid such figures of speech as *Pandora's box, right up his or her alley, a lick and a promise, blowhard, prickly heat,* and the interrogatory *Come again?*

2. When referring to characters who are or have been in prison, watch your spelling of *penal.* It is NOT *penile!*

3. Flights of metaphorical prose are not desirable. The phrase *her oleaginous Mountain of Venus* only perplexes many of our readers. We were distressed recently to receive a letter that angrily asked: "What's that statue doing up on a hill with butter all over it?" *Wet cunt* is much better.

4. The following have been declared obsolete by *The Dictionary of American Slang:* quiff, quim, hair pie, muff (noun and verb), knockers, and wink.

5. To avoid alliteration, onomatopoeia, and unintentional rhyme, do not name any characters Peter, Dick, Rod, or Regina.

6. The word *vector* is a physics term pertaining to a straight line and is not generally known. Call your penis something else.

7. As you know, printing errors cost money. Using the British expression *John Thomas* for penis recently resulted in a regrettable incident in final page proofs when we discovered this example of anthropomorphization: *"Gimme a cigarette, baby,"* said John Thomas. Remember we are all Americans here.

8. When writing Lesbian sex scenes, irredeemable chaos often results from the plethora of female pronouns that must of necessity be employed. To wit: *"She tickled her clitoris, and with a scream she threw her legs around her hips and dragged her down on top of her."* We suggest that Lesbian lovers be of different coloring, so that one has blond pubic hair and the other brunet. That should help keep your characters straight.

9. Our proofreader is required to read the galleys and page proofs of twelve books a month. Please do not make her burden heavier with tricky sentences. We refer to a recent description of a musician hero who had learned "to master Beethoven." The proofreader automatically changed it to read: "to masturbate often." Remember that we think along certain lines here.

10. Although we require young characters and contemporary settings, please remember to supply your women with garter belts. THIS IS VERY IMPORTANT!

11. *Areola* is the pink area around the nipple; *aureola* is a synonym for halo. Kindly learn the difference.

12. Get right into the action on page one. Leisurely descriptions of scenery and setting are always fatal. Our readers don't care where anybody is.

That evening, after Polly and I got back from ROW, I locked myself in my room to begin my career as a professional pornographer. For the first time in months I didn't feel blocked—what was there to be blocked about? No plot, no characterization, no dialogue except grunts and groans and four-letter words. I would write a book a week and save my money until I had enough to quit, move to New Orleans, and write a *real* book.

My first task was choosing a pen name. I entertained a fleeting temptation to call myself Brad Shaw, then reluctantly cast it aside. Samantha was monitoring Sword & Scabbard's list so I had to pick a name that gave no hint of my identity. The bylines on the two books Amy had given me were I. M. Bigg and Kandy Kuntz, so I decided to be Pussy Slick.

The associations came readily after that. I decided to write about a girl who goes on a picnic with six men and ends up as the entrée. I rolled a sheet of paper into my typewriter and composed the title page.

BOX LUNCH

by

Pussy Slick

The next page was harder. I was used to Regencys, where women never got anything kissed except their hands. Gothics were equally pristine: the hero never touched the heroine except to pull her out of an abandoned well.

Nor were the sex scenes in my favorite novels any help, chiefly because there weren't any sex scenes in my favorite novels. *Ethan Frome* is about a man who never got a piece and *On the Eve* is about a man who got a piece and died.

Then there was the Ayn Rand sex scene in which the characters decide to hump because they both love the gold standard. An Ayn Rand romp could get pretty steamy but there was always an air of I-wouldn't-do-this-with-just-anybody that was bound to offend the porn reader's fragile ego.

There was nothing to do but forget my own preferences and begin. My fingers found the keys and I wrote my first sentence:

"She pushed her cunt against his face and he licked it with a loud slurp."

Style, said Flaubert, is everything.

Two hours later, I had done thirty pages. I was rolling number thirty-one into the typewriter when I heard the faint, faraway sound of our telephone, followed by the usual jogging noises as Polly started on her sprint. She caught it on the ninth ring.

"ISABEL!"

I went out onto the landing and leaned over the banister.

"WHAT?"

She waited until my echo faded and yelled again.

"IT'S FOR YOU! IT'S YOUR AUNT!"

I raced down the steps, across the dim foyer, through the pitch-black dining room, and into the kitchen. Polly handed me the receiver and I collapsed panting, in a chair.

"Hello, Aunt Edna? Is anything wrong?"

"Law, no, honey! Everything's *right!* I'm calling to tell

you the wonderful news. I'm with child by Virginius!"

I made a strangling sound. She meant the Reverend Virginius Madison Chillingsworth, rector of St. Jude the Impossible, whose secretary she had been for almost as long as I could remember. I didn't know she had been anything else.

"Father Chillingsworth?" I croaked.

"Yes! And he's so happy!"

He was so married, too. "Are you going to have an abortion?"

"'Deed not! I'm going to have a baby!"

"But Aunt Edna, you're forty-one."

"Better late than never."

"Are you sure you're pregnant?"

"Course, I'm sure. I haven't had the Vex of Venus for three months. I've been to seven doctors, just to get a second opinion, and they all said the same thing. I've had the rabbit test and the frog test and every other kind of test and they all came out positive. Isn't that grand? Oh, I just can't wait to see you!"

"See me?"

"Yes, I'll be in Los Angeles tomorrow morning. When I read your last letter I thought it sounded like a right good bunch you've got out there, so being that I'm liberated and all, I've decided to throw in my lot with the Don't Tread on Me Commune!"

"Give me your flight number; we'll meet you at the airport."

When I hung up, Polly's ears looked like pitcher handles. I told her the incredible news.

"Beautiful!"

The missionary glow was back.

9

"Flight Four-oh-one from Dulles now arriving at Gate Fifteen."

"That's it!" Polly said eagerly, jumping up from the bench.

She had to reach down and pull on me to bring me out of my daze. I stumbled after her, still unable to cope with this latest and most bizarre turn of events.

Try as I might, I could not imagine a pregnant Aunt Edna. It wasn't just that pregnancy interferes with menstruation and I could not imagine a nonmenstruating Aunt Edna. It was something else: she simply wasn't the intercourse type. Not that she was one of those pathetic creatures the South calls a "poor thing." She was very pretty and had always had lots of dates. The house was always full of her beaux—in fact, one of them had been at the table the night Mama choked to death. But they were always beaux, never heavy love affairs. She used to go out with several men at a time—i.e., the same evening—on group dates to square dances or baseball games, as though she were seeking safety in numbers. She also had a knack for remaining friends with them long after they had married other women, and then she even made friends with their wives. Never once in these odd arrangements had jealousy reared its head. Sensuous women never behaved this way, so I had taken it all to mean that she was either a virgin or something very close to it.

And now she was pregnant by Father Chillingsworth. . . . I wondered if he had seduced her in that smooth satanic way of Episcopal men of the cloth. Or had he used techniques acquired earlier in life, when he played tackle for William and Mary? And what of Mrs. Chillingsworth, a holy terror if ever there was one, the classic hunt matron who was perfectly capable of kicking the dogs out of the way and killing the fox with her bare hands?

"Do you see her?" Polly asked, as the passengers started coming down the ramp.

Like me, she was looking for the woman she had seen in my family photos: the Southern woman who strove for prettiness rather than chic. A bow here, a ribbon there, a bunch of artificial flowers pinned to a belt—all the busy touches of traditional femininity.

We were not looking for someone in a poncho with Gloria Steinem hair, so Aunt Edna was upon us before we saw her.

"Heah I am—both of us!"

We fell on each other and went completely regional, greeting one another in full throat. Aunt Edna screamed "Oh, Law!" and I screamed "I just can't believe it!" and then we both screamed something wordless and pert along the lines of "Yeeeeeeeeee!" which means: *Look, y'all, we're high-spirited!*

Everyone in the airport looked, including Polly, who seemed rather overwhelmed, like all Yankees at such times. I introduced her and Aunt Edna promptly screamed again.

"I knew it! I just knew it! The minute I saw you I said to myself I said that's Polly! 'Deed I've just heard so much about you! Why, Isabel's letters are so full of Polly-this and Polly-that, I feel like I know you already!"

"I'm glad to meet you," Polly said inadequately. "Did you have a good flight?"

She was expecting the conventional "Yes, fine," but she didn't get it.

"Law, no! I thought I was going to miscarry, 'deed I did! It was bump-bump-bump all the way! Just bump-bump-bump! That's no way to treat a *bearing* woman! I'm going to get Isabel to write that old airline a letter—she's such a good letter-writer, don't you think? I always did say she had a special touch—and tell them they almost brought on my baby!"

By now the whole airport knew she was pregnant. It was just like back home when she roamed all over town announcing the onset of her menses. Passengers hurrying by kept staring at her stomach.

"Give us your baggage check, Aunt Edna. We'll get your things for you."

She calmed down at once and gave me a limpid look and laid her hand on my arm.

"There's something about my baggage you should know," she began in a tremulous voice. "I hope it doesn't upset you or bring back memories, but I thought I might as well go ahead and do it. After all, they were just sitting there in that old place all this time, so I figured that since we pay the storage on all that old stuff, and since it belongs *rightfully* to you by law, I just might as well do it. So, to make a long story short, I did."

Polly was leaning forward in a tilt of curiosity, straining for the end of the long story made short. It was just the response Aunt Edna wanted. She paused dramatically and sucked in her lower lip.

Polly took the bait. "Did what?"

Yankee directness only encourages the Southern woman's thespian instincts. Aunt Edna now laid her hand on Polly's arm.

"Do you know about Isabel's father . . . I mean, how he went?"

"Yes," Polly said uncomfortably.

"That's good. I believe in clearing the air and coming right out with things, instead of keeping it all secret. There's no sense in hiding it because it always comes out eventually, don't you think?"

So far, we hadn't moved from the spot where we first sighted each other. People were swarming and churning impatiently around us but it had no effect whatsoever on Aunt Edna's narrative style; like all Southern women, she was a *succès fou* as an oral historian.

"Besides," she went on, "I thought it would be a nice way to honor poor Fax. It would please him more if I were traveling by ship, but nobody does anymore. So anyway, to make a long story short, I *used* them. As I say, they belong to Isabel when you come right down to it, and there wasn't any point in just letting them sit there in that old place, so I decided to do it."

"Why don't we get your baggage," Polly suggested. "Then you can tell us about . . . whatever it is you want to tell us."

"But that's what I'm talking about, honey!" My baggage! I wanted to warn Isabel about it first so as not to upset her or bring back bad memories. You see, I packed everything in poor Fax's hatboxes."

Polly nearly collapsed with relief when the denouement finally emerged. We went to the baggage circle and there, coming through the rubber straps, were Daddy's greatest business disaster, clogging up the flow of all the smart new Touristers and Guccis and Val-A-Paks and causing no end of curiosity among the many California swingers who had never laid eyes on a flowered hatbox in their lives.

"How many do you have, Aunt Edna?"

"Thirty-seven. I needed a lot because I brought a whole layette for the baby besides my own clothes."

Three exorbitantly tipped skycaps later, we had all the hatboxes in the back of the van. The long drive home was made to order for Aunt Edna's story of her ecclesiastical love affair, but wanting the largest possible audience for it, she chose to save it until we got to the commune. To fill up the road time, she regaled us with a long-drawn-out story about something else. Since the longest-drawn-out stories in Queen Caroline are invariably about Kissypoo Carmichael, she told one. Polly almost sideswiped a truck when she heard the name.

"Why on earth do they call her that?" she asked.

"That's what her *daddy* called her," Aunt Edna explained with heavy sarcasm, "so she won't answer to anything else. She was under her daddy's thumb like I was under my mother's!"

Her voice turned uncharacteristically bitter when she spoke of Granny. I looked at her with curiosity. This was a new Aunt Edna; some change that went deeper than her Gloria Steinem look had come over her.

We arrived at the house. She greeted Agnes, Martha, and Gloria with another cascade of I've-heard-so-much-about-you's; then we all gathered around the table for coffee and an unabridged account of the romance of the century.

"Virginius and I have been intimate for many years," she began. "It started when Isabel was twelve. Of course, we were always discreet. I believe in being discreet. That's why we never went to motels or anything trashy like that. It always happened on church property. In the robing room. To make sure we weren't caught *flagrante delicto,* we did it in the vestment closet."

"With all those heavy brocaded chasubles?" I asked.

"The curtains of charity, honey. We just made a space

between Epiphany and Pentecost and fell into each other's arms."

Agnes's eyes widened. "Did his wife find out?" she asked in hushed tones.

Aunt Edna let out a delighted hoot. "Law, no, darlin'! Babe Beaufort was always up in Warrenton ridin' that damn horse. That's how come Virginius was able to ride me!"

I couldn't believe it. Uninhibited as she was in so many ways, I had never heard her use a cuss word or a bawdy expression. A moment ago, she had circumlocuted her way through *flagrante delicto,* and now she was tossing off double entendres about riding. It was as if two Aunt Ednas were before me, the old one and the new one, taking turns.

"Who is Babe Beaufort?" asked the thoroughly bewildered Polly.

"Virginius's wife. Beaufort was her maiden name. Her Christian name is Charlotte but she's always insisted on being called Babe." She engineered a trenchant pause and rolled her eyes. Now we were back to the old, coy Aunt Edna.

"What's that supposed to mean?" I asked.

"She's a dyke."

The word came off her lips as flat as a knife blade. I was so stunned that for a moment I couldn't remember what a dyke was. As I struggled to form my next question, the new Aunt Edna receded and the old one came back to tell the rest of the story in standard Queen Caroline style.

"Well, you know how she always stamped around in those boots, and wore britches in church, and carried on like a hussar. Everybody knew Virginius married her for her money, but nobody thought a thing of it—Episcopal priests always marry money. She would have stuck out like a sore thumb anyplace else but Virginia, but we're so used to those crazy women runnin' around yellin' and wavin' whips that we didn't know there was anything wrong with her. Course, Virginius knew that all wasn't well in the boudoir. He said she went stiff as a board every time he touched her, so finally, he just stopped touchin' her. That's where I came in—I *melted* when he touched me!" She sighed happily. "Meanwhile, while *I* was meltin' in the vestment closet, *Babe* was meltin' up in Warrenton."

She broke off and turned to me. "Isabel, you 'member that other horsey woman, the one that shot the lawyer from the Anti–Blood Sports Society? Her name is Josepha Cunningham but she likes to be called Dutch." Here she lowered her eyes and sucked in her lower lip.

"She and Babe are lovers," Polly guessed.

"For years!" Aunt Edna caroled happily. "That's how come everything's worked out so beautifully for all four of us! See, when I told Virginius I was pregnant, he decided to ask Babe for a divorce, money or no, but before he could do it, *she* came to *him* and confessed the whole story about how she and Dutch have been in love all this time. She said they went to a N.O.W. consciousness-raising meeting and talked about Lesbianism and all, and decided it was time for them to come out of the closet and live together openly. So that means that Virginius and I can come out of *our* closet and get married! Isn't that just grand? Hooray for Women's Lib!"

Polly's triumphant grin spread slowly over her face and locked practically behind her ears.

"The divorce is in the works now," Aunt Edna went on. "It'll be final in time for us to be married before the baby's born."

"Will there be any problem for Virginius in the church?" I asked.

"Oh, that reminds me! I forgot to tell you about his interview with the bishop!" She turned to the others in explanation. "You've got to know what the bishop is like before you can appreciate this. You know the Pope? Well, imagine somebody who's more Catholic than the Pope, only he can't admit it because he's an Episcopalian. Everybody's been expecting His Grace to do a Cardinal Newman for years now. Frankly, I think he should go ahead and convert before he loses his mind. That happens, you know, in the higher Anglican circles. The theological doubts just build up and build up until finally they go kaflooey."

Martha, used to clergymen who never had theological doubts, was starting to look a little confused.

"Besides," Aunt Edna continued, "His Grace must be eighty if he's a day. He ought to resign and let the new brooms of modernism sweep out all those old cobwebs. Virginius would make a wonderful bishop—purple's his best color. Anyway, to make a long story short, His Grace called Virginius in and said: 'Do you think a priest of the Anglican Communion should be a divorced man with two wives living?' That's the way he talks. And do you know what Virginius said? He said: 'Your Grace, if it weren't for divorce, there wouldn't *be* an Anglican Communion.' "

Now Gloria grinned—the first really alive expression I had ever seen on her face.

"He sounds cool," she said. "I'd like to meet him."

"He'll be here in about three months. He's getting a leave of absence so he can be with me when the baby comes. That'll give things time to blow over in Queen Caroline, too." She looked around at us brightly. "I hope y'all don't mind if I have the baby here?"

"Not at all," I said. "You couldn't be in better hands. Polly knows everything about birthing babies."

Aunt Edna's arrival was a dream come true for Polly; at last she had somebody to fill out forms with. No clin-

ic, center, or workshop was too avant garde for my new-
ly liberated kinswoman. The two of them huddled for
hours talking knowledgeably about amniocentesis, the
pros and cons of the ultra-sound test, and which Lamaze
Method group was better than some other Lamaze
Method group. I gave thanks that we had broken the
birth bucket; Aunt Edna had grown so broadminded that
she probably would have given that a try, too.

The house was strewn with what Polly called literature: brochures on the papaya-seeds-for-heartburn
movement, pamphlets on how to breathe, folders on
how to pant, flyers announcing the formation of a Fluids
Seminar, and a prospectus ominously entitled "Beyond
Lamaze." It made me think of Ariadne running through
the labyrinth with Polly running behind her saving the
string.

The changes in Aunt Edna's vocabulary continued to
amaze me. Cusswords and double entendres were only a
beginning; now the language of liberated whelping
poured from her lips. Gone were the Southern idioms she
used to favor on the rare occasions when she had spoken
of such matters. "Afterbirth" and "nursing" were now
replaced by "placenta" and "breast-feeding," and once
she even said "lactation." Inevitably, she also picked up
Polly's fractured English. When I heard her talking about
"birth-defected" babies, I got homesick for "simple-
minded."

While Aunt Edna and Polly concentrated on what
comes out, I shut myself in my room and concentrated
on what goes in.

My career as a pornographer blossomed. I finished my
first book, *Box Lunch,* in nine days. Amy and Bill loved it
and promptly issued me a check for fifteen hundred dollars. They wanted another book right away, so I produced *Ripe for Plucking,* about a girl in a migrant labor
camp.

"I never thought there was such a thing as the poor man's Erskine Caldwell," said Bill when he had read it, "but you're it."

I got another fifteen hundred for *Ripe.* I put most of it in the bank to replenish my dwindling balance and used the rest to buy a new electric typewriter with an automatic underline key for all the screams and moans that required italics.

Next came *Two Thighs to the Wind,* written in five days. Amy and Bill were so delighted with it that they asked me if I thought I could do a gay boy book.

"We're always short on them," Amy said. "The straight male authors are afraid to write them, the straight women say they don't know how, and our Lesbian authors refuse to write them for some reason I've forgotten."

I was so intoxicated with my quick success and money I was convinced I could do anything, and since anybody in that mood *can* do anything, I came up with a saga called *Forever Umber.*

"Oh, that's adorable!" Amy squealed.

I had come to the conclusion that she was as schizy as Aunt Edna. No matter what hairy perversions we had to discuss in the line of professional duty, she always sounded like a wholesome midwestern sorority girl whispering in the dorm after lights-out. Or maybe it was a case of innocence being its own protection.

A fashion designer by training, she took a special interest in the book covers, and she did the layouts for mine herself after I inspired her with my next subtle examination of the human spirit, *Knockers.*

"I don't care if the *Dictionary of American Slang* says it's obsolete," she said, "it's a great title and we're going to keep it. I've got the jacket design all figured out. The O and the C are going to have little nipples in them. It's just darling. If you want to do a sequel, I can do the same thing with *Boobs.*"

I did *Boobs* in four days and Amy outdid herself with the cover. After I picked up my check, we decided to celebrate with a drink at the cocktail lounge across the street. We left the office and walked down to the corner. While we were waiting for the light, the strains of "Abide with Me" played on a calliope suddenly filled the air. I looked around at the Gnostic Church of the People but it had no bell tower.

"It's the Born Again Good Humor Man," Amy explained, pointing to an ice-cream truck in the intersection. "He's always around."

As it passed us, I saw the slogan *Come as a Child* painted on its side, surrounded by a host of popsicles. The associations were instantaneous.

"*Come Truck!*"

"Oh, that's super!" Amy said. "Like a Sexmobile, right?"

"Yes. The heroine drives around town and does everybody."

"Perfect! When can we have it?"

"I'll bring it down next week."

With the editorial conference out of the way, we went into the cocktail lounge and had our drinks.

Amy hoisted her Bloody Mary. "I have a suggestion to pass on to you," she said. "Bill says you should include some rimming scenes in your books. We were talking about it yesterday and I nearly died! Mary Beth didn't know what it meant and poor Bill had to *explain* it to her. He didn't go into the gory details, he just said 'analingus' and waited for her to catch on. Finally she did, and said 'ugh.' My sentiments exactly."

She frowned suddenly as if she were in the midst of some private battle with herself. After a moment, her eyes grew large with impending confession. She looked around stealthily, then leaned across the table and spoke in a whisper.

"The guy I live with thinks I'm rarin' to go all the time

just because I work for a porn company. But I'm not. In fact, I'm almost frigid, thanks to Sword & Scabbard. I used to have orgasms but now I can't make it no matter what he does to me."

Suddenly, I remembered something I had sensed about the situation at Sword & Scabbard during my first visit. Bill was a good-looking married man of forty and Amy was a sexy single, but they were not sleeping together. Nor, I was certain, had they ever even given it a thought. In any other office they would have had something going, but not at Sword & Scabbard. The peculiar nature of their editorial conferences ("What's a synonym for clitoris?") had killed all attraction between them.

"Sex isn't sexy," I maximed, imagining Polly's pensive frown.

"You can say that again! Have you had any trouble coming since you started writing these books?"

"I don't really know; I'm celibate at the moment."

"Lucky you," she sighed. She thought a minute, then: "Have they made you horny?"

"Not yet."

"Well, don't worry, they won't. In this business, things get worse instead of better."

I didn't believe her. Nothing could dim my enthusiasm for writing porns as long as I was making so much money. After all, if I didn't have a sex life to ruin, what else was there to worry about?

The first hint of trouble came three weeks later, after I had finished an oral opus that included *Come Truck, Eating Out,* and *Getting Head.*

One evening, Polly, who never cooked, took a notion to surprise us. She arrived home with something—she would not say what—in a huge corrugated bag and made us all stay away while she took over the kitchen.

Finally, she called to us that dinner was ready and I went in to see what she had concocted. I couldn't imagine what on earth she could possibly have cooked; there were no aromas and no heat coming from the stove. In fact, the whole kitchen felt oddly chilly.

"Look!" she said, pointing proudly with an icepick. "Raw oysters!"

I clapped my hand over my mouth and ran for the bathroom, but of course I didn't make it. It was like running for the telephone.

After that, the porns started getting on my nerves and the inevitable happened: I began to indulge in what the trade calls "Fucky Fudging."

If you will look closely at a paperback porn, you will find that it has an inordinate number of end pages front and back. End pages are the blank sheets on which you write your name or paste your book plates; authors of decent books autograph them on the end pages. Most books have only one set of them, but porns have something approaching a ream in order to make the book look thicker than it actually is.

In the back, you will also find a complete list of the company's titles, along with a coupon or order blank so that you can buy directly from the publisher. These ads take up several more pages and add to the thickness.

Now turn to the end of any chapter and you will find that it is followed by a blank page. There are anywhere from ten to twelve chapters in the average porn, so that many blank pages can be inserted.

Finally, investigate the dropped chapter headings. These are the words *Chapter One, Chapter Two,* etc. Chapter heads are always dropped a bit, except in *Gone with the Wind,* where they came right up to the top of the page. That's because the book was so long that the publisher had to save space. Porn publishers have the opposite problem: they have to waste space because their exhausted authors start writing less and less bigger and bigger on more and more paper—i.e., Fucky Fudging.

There are many ways to do it. First, you can drop your own chapter heads, saving the editor trouble at the layout stage. Simply roll the paper as far down as your conscience will allow—say five inches from the bottom—and begin.

Next, pepper your story with newspaper headlines, ads, movie marquees, and signs so that you can center them and double space around them. Like this:

BEAVER SHOTS

After you get the sign painted, have your character stare at it for a while, unable to believe what he sees because he's doped up and temporarily afflicted with double vision. Then have him close one eye and reread it so that you can repeat the sign:

BEAVER SHOTS

Fucky Fudging is why porn characters, who show no caution in life's larger moments, always read labels with such meticulous scrutiny:

K-Y JELLY

It is also what makes them such staccato, monosyllabic types with that curious tendency to echolalia that runs through the genre. The more they repeat themselves, pause, think, and start over, the more paragraphs you can indent:

She's a natural blonde, he thought.
A *real* natural blonde.
Was she ever!
"Wow," he breathed, as he stared at her pussy.
There was no mistaking it.
No way!
"Honey," he said, "you're a real natural blonde."

For the same reason, they also interrupt themselves, trail off in the middle of sentences, and drop things:

Brad wondered if . . .
No, no, she couldn't possibly want to be bungholed.
And yet . . .
She knelt down and spread her cheeks.
"Margo," he said, "I—"
The drink slipped out of his hand and crashed to the floor when he saw the jar she had brought from the bathroom:

VASELINE

When I first started writing porns, I put the groans, moans, screams, and grunts in italics. Then I discovered what all porn hacks eventually discover: capital letters take up more space:

"I'MMMMMMMMM COMMMMMMMMMMMM—
IIIIIIIIIINNNNNNNNNGGGGGGGGGGG!"
"YESSSSSSSSSSSSSSSSSSSSSSSSSSSSSS!"

You can do a lot with "yes." Handled properly, it takes up a whole line.

And then there's no. Ordinarily an unpopular word in porn, it is acceptable when the heroine is an initially reluctant virgin, which is often.

"NOOOOOOOOOOOOOOOOOOOOOOOOOO!"
"Am I hurting you?" he panted.
"YESSSSSSSSSSSSSSSSSSSSSSSSSSSSSSSS!"

Normal pain is suggested with "Uh," which, of course, becomes "UHHHHHHHHHHHHHHHHHHHHH!" Abnormal pain, like the kind caused by sodomy, is "Ngh,"

which .... tightly ....translates into ....
"NNNNNNNNGGGGGGGGGGGGHHHHHH!"
Do enough of this and you're at the bottom of a page
in a trice.

You also turn into a twitch. Most porn hacks cherish
the hope of becoming real writers someday, so there
comes a point when you start to fight back in obscure little ways. Since plot, characterization, imagery, allusion,
tragedy, and comedy were all taboo, I took refuge in ma-
niacally elegant grammar. It made me think I was writing
well to have my pimps and sluts and degenerates say
things like:

"On whom did you go down?"
"His cock is not so large as Bob's."
"I have fewer rubbers than I thought."
"If this be the clap, I'll kill you."

I was fooling no one but myself; pornography is virtually a synonym for bad writing. The pornographer's first
rule—genitals must be described in minute detail—results in cascades of adjectives guaranteed to destroy con-
trolled prose. I realized just how bad matters had become
the day I left a note for the electrician:

The fuse at the top with the pointy red shiny glass
covering that swells into a bulbous mass underneath
has emitted sharp, crackling, staccato sparks whenever
I turn on the round button with the deeply depressed
circular rim on the left side of the heater.

Around this time, I came across an anti-porn essay by
Pamela Hansford-Johnson, who claimed that the literary
worthlessness of porn can be proved by transposing its
style to a description of the boiling and eating of an egg.
I gave it a try and came up with this:

I took the glistening, virginally white oval out of the
fiercely bubbling cauldron of hot, hot, hot water and

cupped my hand around it, feeling its contours with sensations of shimmering delight. I reached for my long, sturdy, battering egg knife and tapped. The shell slipped off and I touched the tender, moist, protein-swollen membranes of the secret softness. The steamy slice of hot, ready, delectable egg burned my fingers but I thrust firmly with my rigid tool and inserted the erect, serrated blade. The lubricious, golden yellow, ambrosial nectar of the pulsating, quickening core gushed out into my egg cup. I centered my mouth over the slickened surface of the gently curving silver spoon and ate, ate, ate.

When I finished this exercise, I stared at my long, yellow, blue-lined Nixonian legal pad in horror.
It was perfect.
Was it ever!
Really perfect.
I was going nuts. . . .
"I'm going nuts," I said.

I guess I had a nervous breakdown. I say *guess* because it did not fit any of the South's nervous breakdown patterns that I had grown up hearing about. I didn't "go to pieces," I didn't "walk up and down the floor wringing my hands and crying," and God knows I didn't "waste away"—my appetite remained as gargantuan as ever, especially now that Martha had taken over as chief cook and was plying us with down-home specialties.
I did not pull any of those high-strung capers that Southerners like to brag about because they make everybody feel aristocratic. Riding a horse through the house is the all-time favorite in this category, but anything Zelda-ish will do. The trouble is, most such goings-on involve appearing in public without clothes, and that's the last thing a disintegrating pornographer wants to do. Nor did I follow in the footsteps of Kissypoo Carmi-

chael, who used to get a faraway look in her eye and whisper, "My daddy loved me best." Whatever else was wrong with me, I was not a Southern child-woman; my daddy loved the *Titanic* best.

Outwardly, I remained the same wonderful girl I had always been—pessimistic, introverted, agoraphobic—so I was a failure as a Southern nervous breakdownee. Thus I suffered a guilt attack on top of my breakdown because I wasn't having the right kind of breakdown. It was like getting a bee sting on top of a snake bite.

I was terrified that I had ruined my writing talent, but there was no one to turn to for help. The Great Helper was incapable of grasping abstract agony, and in any case I could not let her know I was writing porn. Aunt Edna was sunk in self-absorption, perpetually running off on her professional madonna rounds to learn How to Stretch or How to Fart. I didn't dare tell Martha I felt nervous for fear she would start identifying with me again and get nervous, too; and confiding in Agnes, our weakest vessel, was out of the question. As for Gloria, she was the most unshockable, but she could turn any subject into a discussion of Edward II's flaming anus, and I had written too many sodomy scenes to endure her favorite topic.

My nights were worse than my days. I dreamed of broken pencils, stuck typewriter keys, and dictionaries with blank pages. I remained in this state for another couple of weeks, until Father Chillingsworth arrived.

10

*The moment Woman sets about doing things for reasons instead
of merely finding reasons for what she wants to do, there is no
telling what mischief she will be at next.*
—George Bernard Shaw

Father Chillingsworth was driving to California. Aunt
Edna stationed herself beside our black desk phone for
four days, not daring to leave the house for fear of missing one of his checking-in calls. Very soon he called us
from Phoenix—he had a most unecclesiastical habit of
driving between ninety and a hundred miles an hour—
and told us he would arrive the next day.

All of us assembled on the veranda to wait for him. In
honor of his arrival, religious Martha had eschewed Agnes's services and gone to a beauty shop for a professional permanent and her bluest rinse yet. I hoped she
wouldn't prostrate herself at his feet; he was a much
stronger cup of theological tea than she was used to. I got
the feeling she expected something extraterrestrial with
an escort of Swiss Guards.

At last we saw his car pull into the drive. Aunt Edna
emitted a view halloo and flew down the hill with arms

outstretched like the girl in *King's Row* hurling herself at Robert Cummings. The differences were twenty years and a decided spraddle; she was now "well along" in her Southern vocabulary and "in her third trimester" in her liberated one.

After a warm reunion at the bottom of the hill, they got into the car and rode up to the house. When my uncle-to-be got out and came toward us, Agnes's jaw dropped in frank appreciation.

"Oh, mercy!"

Virginius Madison Chillingsworth was breathtakingly beautiful in the lace and brocades of the Anglican ritual. Out of them, as now, he was merely handsome. At fifty-seven he had silvery temples and the apple-cheeked, carefree look of a man born with a little money who had married a woman with a lot of it. Slightly over six feet, he was massively built, with huge hands and a thick tuft of graying chest hair peeking through the open collar of his sports shirt.

With Aunt Edna clinging to him, he came up the steps, kissed me on the cheek, and shook hands with the communards. Only Polly, who had a number of ministers in her own family, behaved normally. The others reacted visibly to his electrifying presence. Martha dropped the barest of curtsies; Agnes went all girlish in her big-woman way—a kind of twisting, scrunching movement as though she were making room for him in bed. Gloria seemed peculiarly entranced in a nonsexual but nonetheless intense way.

"Well," he said, his glance sweeping around. "Here are all the lovely ladies I've heard so much about, all waiting to greet me. It's indeed a privilege to be so graciously received."

That's when Polly reacted. I never thought I would see her eyelashes flutter, but they did.

While Aunt Edna was showing him their room, Martha heaved a nostalgic sigh and stared off into space with a mesmerized smile on her lips.

"He's just like Roosevelt."

By dinner time, she was calling him Virginius without a trace of embarrassment. He had brought us a huge Smithfield ham, and the two of them discussed country cooking, a subject guaranteed to bring Martha out of her shell.

Next he devoted himself to Gloria, with reminiscences of his trip to her beloved Mont-Saint-Michel, and an obscure little note about the Albigensian heresy. Together they spun it into the finest silk, yet in a way that did not shut the rest of us out.

All of the table talk went the same way. For the first time in nearly a year, we all remained steady on course, with none of the wild lurches into our various monomanias that had characterized our all-female conversations. Polly was actually talking instead of promulgating, and once she even laughed when Virginius told a story about a dogfight that erupted while he was performing the prehunt ritual known as the Blessing of the Hounds.

I decided that there was nothing like having a yang around the house to balance off our excess of yin.

A week later, he and Aunt Edna were married in a discreet ceremony at the house by a Los Angeles rector who had gone to divinity school with the bridegroom. In view of Aunt Edna's condition, the traditional description, *Spinster,* did not appear on the documents after her name. Farnsworth bellowed throughout the service, but otherwise the occasion was marked by that ineffable civilized touch that Virginius cast forth like incense.

He became the first man to spend his wedding night in a feminist commune. The next day, Aunt Edna enrolled him in Husbands' Class, where he learned how to place pillows, time pains, crank up an articulating bed, and "coach" the whole business when the time came. He even consented to taking part in a seminar Polly turned up called Supportive Panting.

Once again life at Don't Tread on Me settled down. Aunt Edna kept the atmosphere jangling, of course, but that was only the outward physical clamor. An inward spiritual grace started to take hold, whose source was Virginius's fireside chats.

He seemed to know that we all had problems. Without being obvious or overly clerical about it, he managed to find time alone with each of us for long, seemingly casual but intensely probing talks. Wandering into the kitchen ostensibly for a cup of coffee, he would settle himself at the table and talk to Martha while she cooked. Next, he would wander down to the beach and help Agnes carry her clam buckets—manna to a woman who was stronger than many men—and wind up in a tête-à-tête on a rotting log.

Polly was usually collating ROW material in the dining room, so Virginius simply got in line and followed behind, helping her assemble the latest bill of attainder while they talked.

Gloria was the most accessible of all, thanks to her habit of squatting on the cliffside and staring out to sea. One day I looked out my window and saw Virginius squatting beside her. Chaucer only knows what they were talking about but it went on for a couple of hours. He was at home in Hebrew and sometimes served as guest cantor at a Richmond synagogue, so they might have been chanting *kaddish* for Edward II for all I knew.

I was the hardest to get to because I worked alone in my room, but one day I heard a tap at my door and found my uncle holding two bourbon highballs.

"I hope I'm not disturbing you, Isabel, but I heard your typewriter stop some time ago, so I decided to see if I could interest you in a break."

We chatted awhile about the latest books—real

books—and then he surveyed me with a pensive air.

"You're looking a little strained, Isabel. Edna and I were talking about you last night. We're worried about you."

The drink was very strong; there are no teetotalers in the Episcopal Church, and Southern gentlemen have a heavy hand with the decanter. Suddenly, I found myself pouring out the whole story of my writing career—and the porns.

"Polly worries about what porn does to women and the churches worry about what it does to the American family. Nobody cares about what it does to writers," I said miserably. "I'm afraid I've ruined my talent for good."

His face had not changed as I talked. There was no shock on it, only concern for me. He tapped his front tooth with his thumbnail, nodding slightly, his eyes narrowing.

"Do you think," he began slowly, "that you might be trying deliberately to destroy your talent to please your grandmother?"

"Granny. . . ?"

"As I recall," he said with a wry smile, "intellectuals were at the top of her long list of enemies. I also recall that she had the strongest personality of anyone I have ever met. A remarkable woman, no doubt, one of the last of the great dowagers. But, I fear, a Know-Nothing and a textbook case of megalomania."

He crossed his legs and lit one of his thin, elegant cigarillos.

"It's taken Edna years to get out from under her mother's yoke. She still isn't out completely and she never will be. One moment she's a liberated woman and the next a Southern belle. I think you've been straddling the same fence. You pleased yourself by leaving home and becoming a writer, yet subconsciously you saw to it that you also pleased your grandmother by not writing anything worthwhile. You told yourself, in effect, that it was permissible to write for a living, to treat it as a job, as long as you didn't treat it as an art and derive intellectual satisfaction from it."

He was right, of course. It was so obvious that I had missed it completely.

"Forever feminine was my late mother-in-law's motto," he sighed, blowing out a cloud of blue smoke. He looked at me with a twinkle in his eyes. "Do you remember the time she donated her womb to the University of Virginia?"

"Vaguely."

"That's when I first began to wonder about her. She summoned me to the hospital and demanded that I bless the womb. It was sitting on the bedside table in a jar. I told her that since I had blessed her many times while it was still in her, I felt it was sufficiently sanctified already, and in any case, I did not bless detached organs. She got very put out with me and sent me away, but the next day she summoned me again. This time she wanted me to accompany the womb on its trip to Charlottesville and conduct a ceremony she had spent the previous night choreographing, to be called the 'Dedication of the Womb.' When I told her that I was not empowered to invent new rituals, she called me a pagan and tried to get me barred from the hospital."

I had never heard any of these details, but that was not surprising; Granny never publicized her defeats.

"But the really intriguing part of the whole affair," he went on, "is that there was nothing wrong with her womb."

My mouth fell open. Virginius nodded.

"I talked to Rex Montgomery about it a few years after he operated on her. There had been some female trouble in the Upton family back in the days of tight corsets, but your grandmother was perfectly healthy in that area. She preferred to believe otherwise, however, so she began persuading herself that she was descended from a long line of fragile flowers who were beset by pelvic demons. Somewhere in the course of all this, she conceived a vision of her womb sitting in a niche at the medical school, the object of a statewide pilgrimage by gynecology students. She decided to donate it to the university, but before she could do that, she had to get at it, so she started plaguing Rex to perform a hysterectomy. At first he refused, but she kept after him until she wore him down. By then she was past the change, so he went ahead and took it out."

"She told me the university begged her to give them the womb," I said. "What really happened?"

"Rex connived with somebody he knew at Charlottesville and got them to write her a letter requesting the donation in the name of science. It was the only way they could quiet her down."

Virginius studied the end of his cigarillo. "That's why I tried to get Edna as much sick leave as I could manage," he said. "I knew her cramps were psychologically induced, but they were severe just the same."

Mine, too, I thought. Oh, Granny, what crimes were committed in your name!

The book in the typewriter was almost finished. I wrapped it up the next day and rode into L.A. with Polly to deliver it and tell Amy that I would not be writing any more.

Polly dropped me at the public library, where I phoned Sword & Scabbard to let them know I was coming and to suggest a farewell celebration before they could make other plans for the evening.

Mary Beth answered the call in a curiously slurred voice.

"This is Isabel. I'm coming in with my latest manuscript. Can you all go out for a drink with me after you close up? There's something I have to tell you."

"Go out?" she giggled. "Don't have to go out. Have a drink right here! C'mon over!"

She had had more than Thom McAn cookies. I couldn't imagine a smashed Mary Beth Cartwright; it was like imagining a smashed Mary Tyler Moore. I hung up and flagged a taxi.

When I arrived, Bill was pouring Mary Beth a Scotch and she was stirring it with her finger. When she saw me, she tried to wave but got confused and stuck her whole hand in the glass. She pulled it out, licked it, and flapped it in my general direction.

"What's going on?" I asked, accepting my glass.

"*Folie à trois*," Bill said. "Now it's *folie à quatre*."

"We all caved in at the same time," Amy explained, knocking back her drink. "It started when the typewriter repairman made a pass at me. He said he figured I must be pretty hot since I work in a place like this, so he asked me to meet him at the motel across the street. He promised me a ten-inch joystick. That's when I started laughing, because we had a book by that name last month. I just laughed and laughed—I couldn't stop. Finally he got scared and left, and I kept on laughing. It was contagious and pretty soon we were all having hysterics. Then Bill went out to the liquor store."

"The old Navy remedy for shellshock," he said, patting the Scotch bottle.

"It's this place," Amy said, hiccoughing. "We can't stand it any longer. It's done us in."

"I wonder what's going to happen to us?" Mary Beth mused. "Sexwise, I mean."

"I can't get it up." Bill shrugged.

"Neither can I," said Mary Beth. "Comparably speaking, I mean. God, I used to dig sex but now. . ." Suddenly she slammed her fist on her desk. "Do you know what my pussy is like? Do you have any idea what my pussy is like? Well, I'll tell you what my pussy is like!"

"Sweetie," Amy said kindly, "you don't have to repeat yourself to take up space. You're not reading galleys now—this is a party. No dropped heads, ha-ha."

"Wait a minute! Wait a minute! I wanna tell you about my pussy. Will you let me tell you about my pussy? About this lubrication business—I don't lubricate like the women in our books."

"Who does?" Amy said. "If I did, I'd get a Pap test before it was too late."

"Wait a minute! Wait a minute! I wanna ask you something. Do you think my pussy is a passion-drenched, quivering, oleaginous, swollen triangle of lubricious lust? Do you think my coral lips glisten with the burning spray of cunt nectar?"

"I hope not," said Bill. "You've used up all your sick leave."

"Do you have any idea what my hair-fringed cloven oval is like? Well, I'll tell you what my hair-fringed cloven oval is like. IT'S AS DRY AS A GODDAMN BONE!"

We all screamed like the hysterics we had become and poured another round. It started to get very hot in the office so I went to open a window. That's when I saw Samantha's car. She was circling the block looking for a parking space; through her hatchback window I saw several cardboard cartons full of mason jars.

"She's coming to throw blood!" I cried. "Lock the doors!"

"Who's coming?" Amy asked blurrily.

"Stop talking dirty!" Mary Beth yelled.

I finally managed to get through to them and explain who Samantha was and what was imminent. Bill recovered first.

"The number," he said. "Call the number."

"What number?"

"The one they gave us to call if there was ever any trouble."

"The police?"

"No, just a number. I don't know whose it is. They just told us to call it."

"Who's they?"

"We don't know that, either," Amy said, reaching for her phone list. She managed to find the number and recite it to Bill, who managed to punch out the right buttons on the phone.

"Trouble at Sword & Scabbard," he said tightly into the mouthpiece. "There's a Honda driving around the block with a radical feminist in it. She's going to attack the office."

He hung up and we all gathered at the window and waited. We didn't have to wait long. In a few moments we heard the strains of a familiar old hymn; then the Born Again Good Humor Man tore around the block on two wheels, aiming his truck straight at Samantha's tiny car.

Glass shattered and steel crunched. Samantha's Honda skidded in a circle in the middle of the street. The Good Humor truck reversed with a squeal of tires and shot forward again, aiming this time for her front end. She kept skidding around and the truck kept going for her like an enraged bull, until all four of her fenders were crumpled like balls of discarded onionskin in a writer's wastebasket. There was blood all over the street; the few Mason jars that hadn't broken were rolling around in the remains of the hatch.

Samantha jumped out and took off down the street on her long, basketball player's legs, her screams drowned out by a church chorus on the truck's tape deck. "Stand up, stand up for Jesus, ye soldiers of the Cross! Lift high his royal banner, it must not suffer loss. . . ." The singing rose up for a moment, then faded quickly as the truck spun around and disappeared down an alley.

"That's who owns Sword & Scabbard," Bill said.

He was not referring to the Mormons. The ice-cream truck had no sooner left than a tow truck marked "DeLucia's Garage" appeared. A man jumped out, affixed a hook under the bumper of Samantha's ruined car, and towed it away. Finally, there came a street-cleaning truck to wash away the blood and glass with foamy jets of water. In no time, all traces of the melee were gone, and there wasn't a cop in sight.

Soon a huge black Buick pulled up in front of the building. Two powerfully built men in pastel Western suits got out and hurried into the entrance.

"Here they come," Bill said.

"Are they going to throw acid on our kneecaps?" Amy whispered.

The door burst open and the pair entered. Both were in their thirties, with shiny black hair and alert dark eyes. The shorter and stockier of the two introduced himself as Gino and seemed to be in charge.

"You guys okay?" he asked us, his jaws working over a piece of gum.

"Nobody came upstairs," Bill said. "It was just the one woman in the car."

Gino's dark face split into a wide grin. "Yeah," he said happily. "You know who that broad was? The one we been waiting for. She's president of that ballbreaker outfit—HOW, NOW, POW?" He turned to his partner. "What the hell is it, Dominick?"

"ROW."

"Yeah!" He grinned again and he motioned us to sit down. He studied us closely.

"You guys all got that look," he began, then nodded in agreement with his own statement. "Yeah, you got that look. Nothing personal, you know what I mean? Everybody who works here gets it. Nobody ever lasts very long." He clapped his palms over his knees in a gesture of finality. Beside me, Amy whimpered.

"Look, folks, we gotta put in a new set. I'm real sorry but like I said, it don't look like you gonna last much longer anyway. It gets to you, working here. The last guy that ran this place shaved off all his hair and went to Tibet. Said he was gonna be a monk. Swore he never wanted to touch another broad as long as he lived."

He turned to his partner and snapped his fingers. "Dominick, the case."

Dominick handed him a tattered black attaché case. When he opened it, I saw that it was full of cash. He wet his thumb and started peeling off bills.

"Let's see, whatta we pay you guys?"

Amy, Bill, and Mary Beth quoted their weekly salaries and Gino paid them in full without question. Then he turned to me.

"I don't work here, I'm a writer."

"She just turned in her latest manuscript," said Amy, holding up my brown envelope.

"That's fifteen hundred, right?"

We nodded and he counted out fifteen one-hundred-dollar bills and handed them to me. Once again, he studied us shrewdly, an amused smile playing on his lips.

"Now, look," he said softly. "You don't have to declare this on your income tax, so don't, okay?" He clapped his hands over his knees again and stood up. He was only about five-six but he oozed dominance and self-assurance.

"You guys got a consolation prize coming," he said. "Come on over to the restaurant and have a nice dinner on the house." He looked at his watch. "Make it in about an hour, okay?"

"What restaurant?" we asked.

"My mother's," he said reverently.

He gave us directions and they left. We made some black coffee and washed our faces and then piled into Bill's car. The restaurant, called "Mamma DeLucia's," was tucked away behind an abandoned 1930s movie palace in a fringe neighborhood full of small businesses and mobile-home lots.

When we entered the restaurant, Gino was seated alone in a large booth, looking as though he was waiting for someone. Amy and I exchanged a glance; we hadn't expected him to be there to receive us, much less to join us, but the table was set for five.

As we sat down, a stout woman with salt-and-pepper hair in a bun emerged from the kitchen and strode over to us with a purposeful air.

"Gino!" she snapped.

He sprang up. "*Si, Mamma?*"

She said something in machine-gun Italian. I caught the words "Lachryma Christi." Gino vanished into the wine cellar and returned with four bottles, two red and two white.

"Tear of Christ," I translated, awed by the twenty-year-old dates on the labels.

Mamma looked pleased and Gino watched me closely with intense interest.

"Ah, you like-a Lachryma Christi?" Mamma asked.

"I've never had any, but I've heard a lot about it."

Her smile broadened. "Now you have some. Gino! Bring-a glasses!"

He shot up again and went to the bar. Mamma returned to the kitchen.

"Talk about assertive women," Any whispered. "She's doing okay."

"Old Ironsides," Bill agreed.

Gino returned with the glasses and slipped into the booth—next to me. We drank wine and talked about sports and movies until Mamma came with the antipasto. Lasagna followed, and it was beyond description. After the meal, we drank more wine and the talk turned to cars.

"I've been looking for a good secondhand car," I said suddenly, thinking of the cursed van.

"You want a car?" said Gino, turning to me with a penetrating stare. "I'll get you a car."

I looked down in confusion and gulped some wine. He chuckled knowingly.

"I don't mean a hot one. This is on the level. I got a cousin that runs a used-car lot up the street. You want me to take you there?"

His eyes were like chips of coal. As we looked at each other, the inexpressible happened: It's called *click*. We began talking on two different levels, the subject at hand, and another one.

"Now?"

"Why not?"

"All right."

We rose. Bill looked worried but I saw Amy give him a jab with her elbow. He looked from her knowing face to Mary Beth's and settled into male confusion. They would explain it all to him after I left.

I shook hands with Mamma. The rings that had fit her when she was a young woman were now embedded in her flesh, never to be removed. Some flour came away from her handshake and that was pleasant, too.

Gino held my jacket, said something to his mother in Italian, and then we walked out into the dark street. We got into his big Buick and drove a block or so in silence. He pulled into a flag-strewn phantasmagoria called "Square Deal DeLucia's" and parked in front of the trailer office.

I reached for the door handle and started to let myself out.

"Sit still," he said, and came around to my side. He

opened the door for me and took my elbow and steered me into the shack.

"Hey, Sal! Gotta customer for you!"

A man at a cluttered desk rose and came over to us.

"She wants a car. Not one of them heaps you got out front. One of the good ones."

"What kind do you want?" Sal asked me.

"She don't know what she wants. You still got that sixty-nine T-bird I was looking at yesterday?"

"Sure I still got it."

"Okay, let's see it."

More steering, some gravel, and a darkened corner of the lot behind the service area. A gorgeous white T-bird that looked brand-new. Gino opened the door and shoved me in the driver's seat, then got in beside me.

"Take a spin, see how it feels," he said, taking out a fresh stick of gum. He tossed the wrapping out the window and folded the stick in his mouth while I started the car. The engine was as quiet as an electric typewriter.

Gino cocked his head and listened appreciatively. "Nice, huh?"

He draped his arm over the seat, his fingers not quite touching my shoulder. Once more we were talking on two levels.

"Very."

"I wanna see that you're took care of good."

I drove out of the lot and headed up the street. Out of the corner of my eye I saw him turn his head and look steadily at me. I wondered why he had picked me instead of Amy or Mary Beth. Had it been my little translation that so pleased his mother? Or had it merely been that my expressed desire to buy a car gave him a graceful exit? Maybe he didn't care which of us he had. Maybe he just wanted a Protestant girl because he had heard we were dirty. It really didn't matter. If this is stereotyping, I told myself, I feel like making the most of it.

"It handles beautifully," I said. Actually it was like driving a 747 but I knew I would get used to it.

"I figured it would. You want it?"

"Yes."

I drove back to the lot and pulled up in front of the shack. This time I waited until Gino opened the door for me.

"Give him eight of them C-notes," he instructed.

Not even Cap'n Nehemiah could have gotten such a bargain. Inside the trailer, I counted out the money and put it on Sal's desk. He said nothing, just nodded and started to make out the pink slip and the temporary tag.

Gino put a coin in the soft-drink machine and pressed the Coke button. The can rolled out and he tore off the tab, took a swallow, and handed it to me. We took turns drinking from it, holding each other's glance all the while.

"What's today's date?" Sal asked.

"The sixteenth," said Gino.

Oh, God. . . . Well, if anything happened I could always fill out one of Polly's forms.

When the paperwork was finished, we returned to the car. More door-holding. Then: "See that shed way in the back near the alley? Drive in there."

It was a tin structure, the kind you buy in sheets and put together yourself. The car just fit into it. I turned off the lights and Gino reached down for the adjustment lever and pushed the seat back as far as it would go. I did the same with mine.

He unbuttoned my blouse. "I'm glad you wear a bra," he said, as he took it off. "I hate these sloppy broads nowadays. It ain't decent."

I wished I had been wearing a dress. Two flies unzipping at once is depressing, however quick. When I started unpeeling my pantyhose I also wished I had on a garter belt. I felt like an onion. That was one thing the porns were right about.

The shed smelled of grease and tar and Gino smelled of something unadvertised—bay rum or perhaps Florida Water. His mouth tasted of spearmint. We passed the gum back and forth with our tongues. "Ladies don't chew gum," Granny had often told me, but she never said anything about playing catch with it.

He pulled me across his lap and settled my knees around his hips. "Never sit in a man's lap because he can feel the shape of your privates through your clothes." Well, that was academic now. What else? "Never linger in a parked car because a criminal might come along and take his pleasure with you." There was no danger of that unless the Bradshaws had repealed the law of averages.

It was quiet except for the noises we were making, all blessedly unspellable. When they stopped, I had the gum.

After a few minutes, he reached down and pulled up his pants. I did the same, and then backed the car out of the shed. I drove over to the office, where he had parked his Buick, and let him out. We looked at each other in the glare of the neon lights. We would not meet again and we both knew it.

"*Ciao,*" he said.

"Bye."

As I watched him walk away, I realized that it was the first time I had ever had sex solely because I wanted it, with no thoughts of gathering experience in the back of my mind. I was still pulsating; for a horrible moment I forgot how to drive. Then I remembered something about depressing the clutch, but there wasn't any.

At last I managed to move forward. I stopped at a pay phone to call Polly at the McGovern for President head-quarters to tell her she didn't have to pick me up.

"I just bought a car."

"At *night?*" she asked, horrified.

"It was still light when I bought it," I lied, and then realized my mistake.

"What have you been doing all this time?"

"I went to an ethnic-awareness meeting."

"I think that's *fine,*" she said stoutly.

11

Men's men. Gentle or simple, they're much of a muchness.
—George Eliot, *Daniel Deronda*

Polly was in her most officious mood when she inspected my new car the next morning.

"A T-bird! They're so *dear*! How could you spend so much money?"

"I had a felt need."

"Hmmm. . . . There's a stain on the front seat. See? That's what I meant when I asked you if you bought it at night. I'll bet you didn't even see it. Well, don't worry about it, I'll get it out with Scrubbi."

I spent the rest of the day smiling the Cheshire cat smile of the just-laid, and the next three weeks enjoying a guilt-free vacation. Heretofore, my vacations had been writing blocks, but now that I knew my professional problems were solved, I was able to curl up with *The Decline of the West* and not worry about a thing. When my period arrived on time and almost crampless, my victory was complete.

Soon Aunt Edna was ready to throw her foal. Virginius reserved a "birthing room" for the two of them at the hospital; she was determined to have natural childbirth, but because of her age, her doctor advised her to arrive early for careful monitoring just in case, so they left for the hospital before her pains started. Virginius, who was going to move in with her for the duration, promised to call us with regular reports and let us know when labor began so we could be there for the event.

The house was strangely empty after they left. It was winter, and the wind whistling in from the sea made the old walls creak and groan. We gathered in Martha's warm, redolent kitchen and, to Polly's despair, swapped old wives' tales.

"They say a baby with older parents will have a high I.Q.," I said.

"Statistics show—"

"They say having a baby late in life delays the change," Martha said.

"Recent research—"

"I hope it comes this weekend. Sunday's child is fair of face," said Agnes.

"If the baby comes at night and there's blood on the moon, make sure you look at it through your legs and spit three times." This, of course, was Gloria's contribution.

Suddenly Agnes cocked her head and listened.

"What was that?"

"What was what?"

"I heard a noise, kind of like a thumping."

"It's the house," said Polly. "I got the appraiser's report the other day and you should see—"

She was interrupted by a horrendous bellow of "BAN-ZAI!" and several gunshots. The thumping turned to heavy footsteps, and then the kitchen door burst open.

Agnes screamed. "BOOMER! OH, GOD! OH, NO!"

I looked into the barrel of the shotgun and then up at the man who held it. For a moment I thought it was General Patton come back from the grave: he had all kinds of things hanging on him—straps holding water canteens, binoculars, a walkie-talkie, a bowie knife, a map case, two crossed bandoliers containing extra ammo, and two extra guns, one over each shoulder.

Under all the paraphernalia he wore a camouflage-print battle outfit, boondocker boots, an Australian bush hat like the man on my ceiling, and a gas mask lodged under his chin. He was at least six feet four and looked entirely capable of doing all the things Agnes had told us about. In short, Boomer Mulligan was a paranoid's paranoid.

The first thing he said was "Ack-ack-ack," which quickly grew into "Awwwwggghhhrrr!" and graduated to "AAAAHHHHHGGG!" It sounded very familiar, a kind of morning sound. I was so terrified that it took me several seconds to realize that he was coughing—with his finger on the trigger. . . . I saw the coroner filling out my certificate. *Cause of death:* 61,345 Raleigh coupons.

At last he recovered and spoke in a hoarse, raspy voice. "You stole my wife," he said accusingly, looking menacingly around the table.

"Boomer, please! Don't shoot!"

"Shut up! You're coming with me, Agnes. I'm gonna— *ack-ack-ack*—make a real woman out of you. Everybody up!" he ordered. "Put your hands on top of your head and walk!"

We rose and paraded in single file out the kitchen door. I was bringing up the rear so I had the gun in my back. Agnes had turned to jelly, but her sobs and pleas moved him not.

"It's no use, Agnes. I'm gonna fuck—*ack-ack-ack*—you. You deserve it."

"How did you find me, Boomer?"

"I got ways."

He herded us into the living room and stopped.

"You," he said, prodding me with the gun. "Pick up that portable TV and bring it."

I did as I was told and he marched us up to the third floor and put us in one of the never-used smaller bedrooms without a bath. He motioned me to put the TV on the bureau and plug it in.

"Turn it on to Channel Seven," he said.

"What's that for, Boomer?" Agnes asked.

"So's you can watch the hostage crisis."

"What hostage crisis?"

"This one, you sap!" The shout caused him to have another hacking seizure. We waited through it until he had stopped wheezing. "I called the TV news people," he went on. "They'll be here any minute."

Still drawing a bead on us, he used his other hand to uncap his water canteen and take a long swig, which he swallowed, and then another, which he gargled and spat out. Clearing his throat, he reached into his cartridge belt and took out a Vicks cough drop and popped it between his grim lips.

He left the room with Agnes in tow and shut the door. I heard him outside, doing something with a chain—apparently he carried one of those, too. When I saw the knob move I realized that he was tying the chain to it and wrapping the other end around the banister.

We heard the two of them going down the stairs to the second floor. From the direction of their footsteps, they were headed for her room.

"That man's crazy as a loon!" Martha sobbed. "What's he gonna do to poor Agnes?"

Before anyone could reply, a commotion sounded from the driveway. Looking out the window, we saw TV trucks pulling up to the house, followed by a police car and an ambulance. Turning to the television set, we saw the same thing, only better. As we watched the screen, we saw some technicians attaching a microphone to a long pole; turning around, we saw it bobbing outside the window.

An on-the-spot reporter kicked off the drama.

"Ladies and gentlemen, we are at the Don't Tread on Me women's commune to bring you complete coverage of the hostage-taking. The terrorist's name is Boomer Mulligan, president of a group that calls itself 'Stop Women's Lip.' I have here a copy of their latest newsletter, *The Wife Beater,* which contains an interview with Mr. Mulligan telling of his plan to capture his runaway wife, Agnes, who fled to the commune. Mr. Mulligan, who is a survivalist, is armed and dangerous and has told WNLA that he has placed explosives around the house and yard."

That did it. At last, I went to pieces. Hurling myself at the window, I screamed into the mike.

"Save the pig! Take him out of the pen! Get him away from here!"

"Ladies and gentlemen, we are getting a statement from one of the hostages. She seems very distraught, but we'll try to interview her. What is your name, please?"

"Never mind me! Get Farnsworth!"

"Ladies and gentlemen, you have just heard the voice of Greta Farnsworth, who's being very courageous about this. You just heard her say 'Never mind me.' "

"You sound like Barbara Frietchie," Gloria said. " 'Shoot, if you must, this old gray head, but spare your country's flag, she said.' "

"I'm not Greta Farnsworth!" I yelled, hearing my own echo from the TV behind me. "I'm Isabel Fairfax and Farnsworth is my pig!"

"We have a correction. The hostage misspoke. Her name is Isabel Fairfax and she just referred to the terrorist as a pig. Standing by in our studio are three members of the National Organization of Women, who are going to discuss female rage."

While the NOWs were venting about venting, I suddenly remembered Quadrupet and threw myself at the window once more. The microphone danced before me but I pushed it aside so I could see into the big oak tree in the side yard. It was Quadrupet's aerie, and as I expected, he was there.

"There him is! Oh, him didn't get him din-dins!"

"Ladies and gentlemen, we have another statement—"

"Fecal-fecal fart-fart, him is mommy's heart-heart!"

The microphone vanished.

"Ladies and gentlemen, we're experiencing some technical difficulties. We now switch you to Lance Gerard, who has located the Don't Tread on Me milkman for a statement on food supplies."

I looked at the screen and there, in the glare of a revolving blue police light, was nice, normal Mr. Willard having his fifteen seconds of fame.

"I would assess that there was sufficient quantity of dairy products so as not to impact anybody very much, should the negotiations reach a stalemate at some prior time."

Next came the two old ladies who lived down the road. We had avoided them after one meeting because they both had total recall of nothing, so they were ideal candidates for the "what were you doing when it happened?" interview.

"I was weeding the garden over by the back fence where the slats are loose when my sister comes out and says, 'I thought I heard shots,' and I says, 'It was probably kids. You know how kids is.' Then my sister says, 'No, it came from that place where they keep the women.' Dinner was ready by then so we set down to the table and my sister says, 'I hear a siren,' and I says 'It's them kids,' but she was sure it was a siren and started to go out and look, but I says, 'You better not go out,' on account of them kids that stole her pockabook last Halloween. You never know what kids might do."

Inevitably, they installed a direct telephone line to the terrorist and interviewed the Ma Bell crisis team that set it up. Telephone installers used to be husky working stiffs who wore their low-lying tool belts with an appealing masculine swagger, but these were stringy, Christlike characters, all eager to interpret the deeper meaning of communication as they had learned it from their company-sponsored course in the psychology of terrorism.

"The breakthrough in negotiations often comes after the direct line is installed," one explained earnestly. "The terrorist needs to feel met . . . like symbolic linkage. . . . The moment of counterintensity follows when the ego is diverted to a sense of outside-worldness in a technological stress-factor reduction."

He was blessedly interrupted by the on-the-spot man.

"Ladies and gentlemen, we are in contact with the terrorist! He is ready to state his demands! Hello? We hear you, Boomer. Go ahead."

"*Ack-ack-ack. . . .*"

"Are you there, Boomer?"

"Yeah. Just cigarettes. I'm tryin' to cut down."

"Can you tell us how your wife feels?"

"She's okay, dumb as ever. Never mind her, it's the country I'm worried about. It's fulla nuts."

"Would you describe yourself as a concerned citizen, Boomer?"

"Yeah."

"Would you like to share your experiences in survival training with our viewers?"

"Yeah."

". . . Well, do you think we're headed for an apocalypse?"

"Nah, but I'll tell you one thing: all hell's gonna break loose."

"What advice can you give to our viewers to help them survive?"

"Shoot to kill."

"Boomer, will you let us speak to your wife?"

"Yeah."

Agnes came on the line with a shrill falsetto keen and complicated the situation at once.

"I'm not the one! I'm not the one he wants! Nobody wants me! I'm Swedish! I'm Astrid Mortensen!"

We exchanged stunned looks. The alias we had concocted for her had not lasted past the arrival of the Raleigh coupon check. After that, everybody had forgotten about it. Apparently, she was in such a panic that she had snatched it out of the blue in some wild hope that it would save her.

"Ladies and gentlemen! We have a new development—"

"We got no new development," Boomer snarled. "This is my wife and I'm gonna fuck her."

What followed was bleeped. "Ladies and gentlemen, Boomer Mulligan has just told us that he is going to have a dialogue with the woman he alleges is his wife."

In minutes we were switched back to the studio, where a grim member of the Swedish-American Society waited to do battle for the Old Norse.

"Ole, were you shocked by Agnes Mulligan's statement that nobody wants the Swedes?"

"Ted, I was. As a member of the watchdog committee I've collected numerous examples of anti-Swedish remarks but I've never heard one so blatant."

"Ole, is the Swedish joke a problem for your group?"

"Ted, we Swedes don't go in much for jokes."

"Ole, I misspoke myself. I meant, do people tell jokes about Swedes?"

"Ted, they might but you wouldn't know it by us. We're serious, hard-working people. The Swedes helped build America. Forty percent of Swedish-Americans who served in this country's wars were decorated for bravery.

Americans of Swedish descent make up the farm popula-
tion of the Dakotas, and that's no joke."

"Py golly," Gloria said. She was standing in the closet
looking up at a panel in the ceiling. "Look, there's a
crawlspace or egress or something in here. I think it leads
to the attic."

We went into the closet and looked up as she removed
the panel. In the dim glow we saw the unfinished tim-
bers of the attic.

"Give me a leg up," she said. "I can go down the back
steps to Agnes's room."

"But Boomer's armed and dangerous!" Polly cried.

She gave us her best troll's smile. "So am I."

Martha and I looked at each other. Had she brought a
knife from the kitchen?

"Gloria, honey, don't," Martha pleaded.

"Help me up."

There was no point in arguing with her. If we didn't
help her, she was perfectly capable of going up the wall
by herself. In her greem rubber boots she had as much
suction as the Human Fly. We joined hands in a cat's
cradle and hoisted her by her foot. She crawled over the
edge of the opening, waited a few moments until her
eyes grew used to the dark, then crept soundlessly off
across the bare dusty floor of the attic.

Some twenty minutes passed. The crowd in the drive
was bunking down on the veranda in preparation for the
"vigil" that the reporter was announcing.

"Ladies and gentlemen, night has fallen here at the
Don't Tread on Me Women's—"

The scream that cut through his words seemed to
shake the house. It was an unearthly sound, like something coming out of a misty bog, so shrill and full of agony that it was impossible to tell whether it was the
voice of a man or a woman.

"Ladies and gentlemen! We've reached a turning

point—" But he was interrupted again when the front door burst open and suddenly there was Gloria on the TV screen.

"Make haste," she cried. "The deed is done!"

Everyone streamed into the house; cops, ambulance personnel, cameramen, and the jabbering on-the-spot newscaster. Someone ran upstairs and broke the chain that held our door closed; it was a fireman with an ax. We rushed out and clambered down the stairs to the second floor with our hearts in our throats, dreading what we would find.

The first person we saw was Agnes, naked as the day she was born, running up and down the hallway screaming about Swedes, Raleigh coupons, and a ransom of freeze-dried disaster food.

Naked except for his Australian hat, Boomer lay on his stomach groaning and coughing at once. His eyes were open in an expression of dumb shock, as though he could not believe what had happened to him. Neither could the horrified newsmen. It took a seasoned Edward II scholar to remain blasé at the sight of Gloria's curling iron sticking out of his ass.

The survivalist had found deliverance. The ambulance attendants wheeled him out on a gurney.

"He raped me!" Agnes screamed. "I don't care if we're married or not, rape is rape!"

She started running up and down the hall again, to the stunned edification of the sixty or so men present. I had never seen her in the nude before. She was really built.

"She's a natural blonde," whispered one of the camera crew.

Polly finally got a robe on her and one of the doctors in our latest entourage gave her a shot to calm her down, but more excitement loomed just around the corner.

Two ominous cars of the type known as "unmarked" tore up the driveway on two wheels each and skidded to a stop just before they went through the veranda railing. Four men jumped out, one of them carrying handcuffs and another a wire-service photo and some other papers. They raced up the steps with a bevy of uniformed troopers behind them and flashed badges at us.

"F.B.I. We've just received word from the director of the Minnesota Women's Prison. The escaped convict, one Astrid Mortensen, is wanted on five counts of armed robbery and murder of a prison guard." He looked at the photo, then at Agnes. "Come along quietly."

"But she's not Astrid Mortensen!" Polly cried, beginning to babble. "We just made that up because of the Raleigh coupons. She's really Welsh but Isabel said she ought to be Swedish, so we picked out a Swedish name for her and used the same initials because Gloria's lover said that—"

"Wait a minute," said the agent. "Are you saying that this woman is not Astrid Mortensen?"

"Yes, of course not!"

"I can prove it," Agnes mumbled sleepily, staggering to her feet. "My driver's license. It's in my bag. I'll get it." She started for her room but the F.B.I. men grabbed her.

I fetched the bag and the men looked at the driver's license. The resemblance between Agnes and the escaped convict was striking, and so were the zaftig vital statistics.

"I'm sorry, ma'am, but you'll have to come down to the Bureau and have your fingerprints taken."

"But the doctor just gave her a sedative," Polly argued. "She's almost out."

"I'm sorry, we can't let her go until we're sure of her identity. You'll have to get her dressed and come with her. If she's the woman Minnesota says she is, she's a real killer."

So we had to dress Agnes. It was like dressing a corpse.

By the time we finished, she was completely unconscious and had to be carried downstairs by four men. The cameras ground away, recording it all while the news reporters got it all wrong. As we made our way through the crush, somebody asked us if Agnes had committed suicide after witnessing her husband's rape.

The F.B.I. would permit only one of us to accompany her in their car. I quickly volunteered for fear Polly would start some sort of political argument. She, Martha, and Gloria followed the government cars in the van.

We arrived at the field office and dragged Agnes in for her fingerprinting. She kept collapsing on the ink pad, until she was covered with smudges that looked like the bruises she had the night we met her. They put the prints on a machine and we all waited. Before long, proof that she was not Astrid Mortensen came spinning out and she was cleared.

But of course it was not over yet. Agnes could get drunk on half of a Pink Lady, so whatever the doctor had given her was bound to have an even more startling effect.

It did. When the F.B.I. man leaned over her to apologize, she came to and gave him a groggy leer.

"I'd like to suck your cock."

He blushed, but before anyone could stop her, she opened her mouth and made a lunging dive for his crotch. Her chair turned over and she fell between his feet and started licking the toe of his shoe. He managed to haul her up but she threw herself into his arms and stuck her tongue in his ear. Several other agents came to his rescue but it was like trying to separate someone from a large, amorous seal.

She kept rubbing herself against whichever agent was nearest. She must have had an orgasm at some point in the fray; by the time we got her into the van, she was limp and peaceful and slept all the way back to the house.

"She won't remember any of it," said Martha.

None of us had the strength to haul her in, so we decided to let her sleep it off in the back of the van. Martha covered her with one of her homemade quilts—we must have been the only feminist commune to hold quilting bees—and we dragged ourselves inside.

Just as we got in the house, the phone rang. It was Virginius.

"I just talked to the television people. They said you were safe but had to go with the F.B.I. Is everything all right?"

"Fine, don't worry about a thing," I said. "How's Aunt Edna?"

"In labor. She was watching TV, and when she saw you singing at the window it brought on the baby."

"We'll be right there."

Virginius met us in front of the birthing room looking like Marcus Welby with a camera slung around his neck. He was scrubbed and sterilized and decked out in operating-room green with a little matching cap.

He had barely greeted us when a familiar view halloo from the birthing room split the air.

"Oh, Law! Here it comes! Virginius, bring the camera or you'll miss the head!"

We heard grunts and pants and Virginius's clicking camera interspersed with "Oh, Law!" and "It's just slidin' like a greased pig!"

A few minutes later there was another sound that made me think of Quadrupet when he had women on his mind. Martha, the only mother among us now that Agnes was conked out in the van, broke into a tremulous smile.

"Oh, Law! I did it! I just did it like I've been doin' it all my life! What is it? Oh, tell me quick." For once she was not interested in dragging out a story.

"A girl!" Virginius cried.

He stuck his head out the door to announce the weight—six pounds, four ounces—and flagged us in.

Aunt Edna was still in position, waiting for either the placenta or the afterbirth, and the baby was lying on her stomach. It would have been embarrassing had it not been for Virginius. Even blood-spattered, he exuded such civilized charm that the slimy baby and Aunt Edna's pudenda seemed like conversation pieces at a rectory sherry party.

The doctor shooed us out so Virginius and Aunt Edna could "experience bonding time." We were all hungry, so we left to have a late supper. Agnes was still out cold in the back and didn't come to until we drove back to the hospital. I waited nervously to see if she had awakened to a new life of nymphomania, but she was her old self again, back to "Oh, mercy." We got her some black coffee and then we all went up to see the baby.

Everyone involved in the birth was now washed and dressed. Aunt Edna, obviously in fine fettle, was sitting up in bed reading a pamphlet on postpartum readjustment.

"I'm going to buy one of those papoose slings called a 'Snuggli,' " she said. "That way, the baby hangs over my front and bumps against my stomach when I walk. That keeps 'em in a fetal position longer and makes 'em think they're back in the womb. It says so right here."

"What are you going to name her?" Martha asked.

"Virginia Mary Upton Chillingsworth."

I wished Gioppi could have been there.

Virginius took a purple stole from his pocket. "I'd like to baptize her now, while everyone is here."

It was another of his perfect touches. There was no need for an immediate baptism; the baby was healthy, but he sensed that we all needed a formal ritual after the disorderly chaos of our hostage crisis. More practically, it was also a means of keeping Aunt Edna from working herself up and demanding to hear a blow-by-blow account of our siege told in exactly the manner she would have told it.

I was the official godmother, but everyone was a sponsor of sorts. To my surprise, Gloria was much more familiar with the responses than I was, especially the ones that appealed to her the most. When Virginius came to "Dost thou renounce the devil and all his works?" she responded with such a vigorous "I renounce them all!" that everyone jumped.

"Wilt thou be baptized in this Faith?" asked Virginius.

"THAT IS MY DESIRE! IT IS MEET AND RIGHT SO TO DO!"

By the end of the rite, Martha was so carried away by Gloria's fervor that she shouted "Praise the Lord!" in the classic Baptist manner. Agnes added a mainstream Methodist "Amen."

Polly looked very peculiar, but then she was a Unitarian. I put her dull eyes and draggy manner down to theology and fatigue, until she groaned and clutched her stomach.

"Look at that child! She's sick!"

Just as Aunt Edna pointed, Polly fell to the floor and rolled over in agony. It was typical of her efficiency to get sick in a hospital; a passing doctor looked in and saw her and called for a cart. They loaded her on it and pushed her down the hall at a dead heat.

"It must be appendicitis," Martha said. "Has she still got her appendix?"

Everyone looked questioningly at me as the original roommate but I did not know. She had never said anything about it, and despite her Bastille-busting efforts for women's liberation, she was very modest, so I had never seen her naked enough to notice a scar.

We waited nervously for the verdict. In a half hour or so, the doctor returned.

"Nothing serious," he said. "Just acute diarrhea."
I leaned so far forward he almost had to catch me.
"Polly?"
"Yep. Never saw a case quite like it, but don't worry.
She'll be okay after a couple days here."

12

Ladies, like variegated tulips, show
'Tis to their changes half their charms we owe.
　　　　　　　　　　　　—Alexander Pope

Two days later, I drove to the hospital and fetched a much looser and even thinner Polly home. I never thought I would see her look so exhausted; not to put too fine a point on it, the Bradshaw had gone out of her.

"I'm going to sell the house," she said suddenly, as we drove along.

"Why?"

"Because it's an awful house. There're about a dozen serious things wrong with it, plus I don't know how many little things. I want to get rid of it before it falls down, and before the taxes eat me alive."

"What about your commune idea?"

She was reaching under herself to rearrange the pillow she was sitting on. "I don't know, I don't care," she moaned. "Oh, God, now I know how Edward the Second felt!"

The next day, the For Sale sign went up and soon lots of friendly, gung-ho realtors with company insignia on their jackets came swarming around with potential buyers in tow, exclaiming over the "wonderful old" tree that was about to fall on the roof. The second most popular shrill was "you could do a lot with," which applied to just about everything.

I was named Sales Drawback of the Year by a realtor who found me sobbing beside the pigpen. The time had come to part with Farnsworth, but I refused to let Polly sell him back to the farmer she had gotten him from for fear he would be eaten.

Once again, Virginius came to the rescue. There was a children's miniature farm outside Los Angeles, something like a Disneyland, run by an interfaith council. It seemed they needed a pig who was used to human companionship and affection so the little visitors could pet it without danger. The job description fitted Farnsworth to a tee, so they came and got him. Another realtor caught me waving at the truck and shouting "Goodbye, precious fart."

Shortly thereafter, Polly got an acceptable offer from a condo developer. By a great effort of will I refrained from suggesting that he call his project Cliffhanger Estates. We had eight weeks to get out, which was just about perfect; by then the baby would be old enough to travel.

After the sale went through, we all gathered around the table to plan our new lives, a task Aunt Edna simplified by inviting everyone back to Virginia. I seconded the motion.

"I own half of the old house, and now that Aunt Edna will be living at the rectory, there'll be plenty of room for five of us."

Polly, Gloria, Agnes, and Martha all hated California by now, so the idea of moving back East appealed to them. The big question was, what would they do when they got there? A few more rap sessions, plus some more fireside chats with Virginius, settled the problem.

The most startling solution was Gloria's.

"I'm going to study for the priesthood," she announced. "Virginius is going to sponsor me."

It was mind-boggling only because the idea of women priests was mind-boggling. Once you accepted the premise that women could lead Flocks as well as flocks, a clerical Gloria made perfect sense. Sweeping across dimly lit stone floors in a cassock was, when you came right down to it, just about the only thing she *could* do for a living.

She now looked respectable enough to get into divinity school. Realizing her Edward II fantasy on Boomer had exorcized her various demons sufficiently so that she had let Agnes cut and thin her hair and agreed to dispense with her drapery skirt. The New Gloria was almost normal, except for certain immutable Old Gloria touches, but that was as it should be: Episcopalians have always preferred the flying buttress to the pillar of church.

As far as I could tell, she wasn't the least bit religious, but she was extremely churchy, and that was far more important. To the Episcopal mind, devout believers are an embarrassing annoyance: the point of it all is to be Christian ladies and gentlemen.

Agnes was going to be Virginius's new secretary. Her stenotyping was now a model of speed and accuracy, so she would be a great improvement over Aunt Edna.

"You'll just love Queen Caroline," Aunt Edna assured her. "It's small, but you don't have to worry, I know everybody for miles around. Come to think of it, there are a couple of very interesting single men I can introduce you to. Now that you're going to get divorced, you can start thinking about getting married again."

Agnes shook her head. "Thanks, but I'm through with marriage. I just don't like being married. I guess it's because I never cared for sex."

We all looked at each other and then thoughtfully contemplated the wall.

Polly and Martha decided to go into business together. They were going to start a Southern fancy foods shop called Dixie Deli, whose specialty would be the (in)famous scrapple. Martha would do all the cooking and Polly would run the financial side. They were very excited about it and already talked of chains and franchises.

Knowing Polly as I did, I knew the enterprise was bound to be a good investment, so I offered them my father's old warehouse and the rest of the hatboxes to get them started. At long last, Queen Caroline would have a Yankee industry and Polly would have a practical outlet for all that Yankee energy.

I assumed that her political spree was over. Since the night of her momentous purge, she hadn't mentioned ROW, George McGovern, free safety-deposit boxes for the poor, I.Q. tests that discriminate against the unintelligent, concerts for the deaf, or the Independent Indian Nation Committee.

Nor did she make a single list. Free at last, I thought to myself.

About five minutes after I thought it, she looked up at Martha over the dinner table and nailed her with the Bradshaw Gleam.

"When we start hiring people for our deli business, I have a marvelous workers' plan I want to institute. My Grandfather Lyman tried to institute it among the Welsh mine owners but they weren't ready for it. Basically, the president of the company serves as president of the union. That way, everyone works together on an equal basis for the betterment of all, and worker-management strife is eliminated!"

I looked at Gloria. "Here we go again. She's going to organize her own labor."

"Jésu. . . ."